Catherine Bruton was born in Cheshire and graduated with a first class degree in English Literature from St Hugh's College, Oxford, in 1994. She has spent time working in Africa as a teacher and for an educational development charity. For the past five years, she has taught English literature and drama at St Paul's Girls' School. She recently became a mother and now lives with her husband and son in south-east London. *Of Silence and Slow Time* is her first novel.

OF SILENCE AND SLOW TIME

August 1914, German Occupied France. When twelve-year-old Amélie stumbles across an injured British soldier in the woods, her family keeps him hidden from the enemy. But the presence of Captain James Winter starts to create suspicion and resentment in the village when he embarks upon an affair with Amélie's sister and attracts the attention of another local girl. As James's activities come under close scrutiny, Amélie becomes an unwitting accomplice. In early 1915, James disappears. Seventeen years later his son comes to the village to find out what happened to his father. Now the secrets of the past look certain to come out . . .

CATHERINE BRUTON

OF SILENCE AND SLOW TIME

Complete and Unabridged

ULVERSCROFT
Leicester

First published in Great Britain in 2004 by
Robert Hale Limited
London

First Large Print Edition
published 2005
by arrangement with
Robert Hale Limited
London

Bruton, Catheri

Copyri Of silence and   e Bruton
slow time /
Catherine
                          LP

1398221

Bruton, Catherine
Of silence and slow time.—Large print ed.—
Ulverscroft large print series: general fiction
1. British—France—Fiction
2. Large type books
I. Title
823.9'2 [F]

ISBN 1–84395–718–3

Published by
F. A. Thorpe (Publishing)
Anstey, Leicestershire

Set by Words & Graphics Ltd.
Anstey, Leicestershire
Printed and bound in Great Britain by
T. J. International Ltd., Padstow, Cornwall

This book is printed on acid-free paper

For Jonny and Joe — my two boys.

France, February, 1932

For me, words are buried in the skin. This is the alphabet I know best: the one I can feel in my fingers, traced on my palm. Not a language of lips and sounds, but the one of lines and touch that James taught me.

Before he came, I was cocooned in a wordlessness, which I had chosen, but from which I could not break out. But now my silence is no longer without words, for his alphabet is etched in patterns beneath my skin, whispering in the shapes my hands can make: the mute alphabet of silence and slow time which he first showed me.

★   ★   ★

Usually, they find them west of here, where the line of the trenches is still scarred into the landscape. But this one they found in the quarry, just a mile from the village, near the ridge. Children, playing hide-and-seek, stumbled on it in their play, and soon the whole village is talking of it. For this one is closer to home and it is one of ours, although there will be some who will say otherwise.

1

I am in the back room when the doctor enters, slicing ham into thin, even slices, allowing my knife to slide slowly through the tanned flesh. Through the doorway, I can see a section of the smoke-filled café; my sister behind the counter; old men I have known all my life playing dominoes in the corner; the soft click of the black oblongs on the wood; my father wiping tables. The day is bright and the café is soaked with light that catches on the coloured bottles in the glass cabinet by which my sister stands, reflecting rainbow streaks upon her white skin, and in the wisps of her hair.

The doctor's voice is flinty, rasping. He speaks through only one lung, the other punctured by a German bullet at Arras. He is one of those who came to the village only after the war, and so he speaks of the body that has been found by the quarry as if it were any other. But I know straight away that it must be James.

I stand at the meat block, the knife still in my hand and I listen.

'They found a body over by the quarry, Leon,' he is telling my father. 'English.'

'Dog tags?' asks my father.

'No.' The doctor pauses. 'They found a cigarette case, with initials.' Then quickly. 'We're going to bring it in.'

They still find them in the fields hereabouts: the bodies of the ones who fell. Every year, some farmer, seated at his plough, feels the hard thud of metal or bone against the rig, and, climbing down to where his straining beast pulls at the bit, finds he has stumbled upon a helmet or a skull, buried beneath the sods. For these are the fields where men died like cattle; in the valley of the Somme, where the river runs by those landmarks whose names have grown just as bloodily notorious: Amiens, Arras, Verdun, Vimy Ridge. The catalogue of loss that war has scarred into the landscape, a vocabulary of death and dying etched in the land, spelling out the names of those who fell in an endless subterranean whispering.

The fields themselves lie still now: the cycle of seed-time and harvest continues on its yearly round. But the furrows of war lie deep beneath, in bleeding pockets where the lost soldiers, ours and theirs, lie like bulbs of death, waiting to spring forth. And every year, one of the lost is found, surfacing like a thing cast up by the ocean as the bloody fields yield up their men.

My father is saying that he will go with the doctor and he is taking off his apron. Two other men rise to join him. I can see my sister, Thérèse, caught in the light from the window, a square of white dissecting her so that her head and torso glow, her blonde fragility almost translucent. She has stopped what she was doing, a cloth in her hand still. She is frozen, her face registering neither recognition nor confusion. I feel a hand on my shoulder and I turn quickly, startled. It is Claire.

She smiles, unaware of what is going on next door, takes my hand in hers and runs her fingers over my palm. I feel their soft, certain touch and in their lines the words begin to form. She smiles at me as she writes and her touch feels like that of her father.

'What are you doing here, standing in the shadows?' her fingers say. 'Spying?'

She is still young, sixteen years old, and yet taller than me, her face an imperfect copy of her mother's, touched less by the extremities of light and shade and thus plainer, but softer also. But there is something about her eyes, which shine as they meet mine, which comes not from her mother and yet seems just as familiar to me and which speaks the same language as the soft, sure strokes her fingers make upon my grained palm.

I take her hand to reply and use the silent alphabet I learned from him.

'They have found another body,' I say.

'Over by the quarry. They want to bring it here.'

'Oh.' She says this with her voice, not her hand, and her tone spells lack of interest. There is no tone in the fingers, only words, and words can sometimes be misread. So her way of speaking is better, more reliable, than the one James taught me. And yet mine is more secret, for she cannot hear what is trapped behind the words I trace on her palm and so she is deaf to the panic that accompanies this news of a body found.

So she turns away, moves to the side where the meat is cooling, runs her finger along the scarred wooden surface. And I do not shatter her indifference.

When a body is found, all the men of the village gather to bury it. They lay it in simple dignity in some remote barn until the official comes from Arras to identify it, if there is enough to identify. Sometimes there are only fragments, shattered, fossilized, barely identifiable as human. Then the broken pieces are gathered, and placed in a wooden box, to be interred in the cemetery in token of a body which lies scattered beneath our harvest.

Sometimes there is a dog-tag or a medal, and a telegram is sent and some still-grieving mother-child-sister-wife, for years having lived with the loss of not knowing, learns what she has long given up expecting to hear. And perhaps there is some relief in the news, in the knowing, or perhaps some long-still grief is messily exhumed to be mourned over again through the silent nights.

The men they find are not often our men. They are English, or German, only occasionally one of ours. But the widows who come, the mothers, sisters, fatherless children, they all appear the same. Similarly confused, similarly untuned by grief. And because we lived with both languages in our midst, the oddly shaped vowels they bring sound as familiar on one tongue as the other and it is hard to remember who was enemy, who ally. For we have our own fatherless children in our midst and some bear English names and others German and yet they play together in the school yard and their names appear side by side with French names in the church register.

I often attend the ceremonies, the mournful little burials. Because each one is representative of the others, the unfound ones; the ones we protected, and those we could not; the ones we feared and yet finally came to see as human. The ones who marched from here to the trenches and did not return; the unfound ones who lie still beneath the sods. I have no words to mourn them with and yet it seems they must be spoken of, and I have no other way.

As I look at Claire, I wonder who will come to grieve this time and what buried secrets will surface when they do.

I hear the door to the café slam to as my father and the other men leave. My sister is alone, behind the counter. I move to the doorway. She has shifted a little so that her face is no longer in the light, and now the lines on her skin are visible. The baby-blondeness of her hair, which Claire has not inherited, looks oddly incongruous next to her face.

I move towards her, out of the shadows, and put my hand upon her arm. I am in the light now and I squint because my eyes are not used to it, and it feels hot upon my skin after the cool of the recess.

Thérèse turns to me and, although she is the elder, I do as I have always done and I reach and stroke the soft blonde tendrils about her brow, my fingers touching her face, reading the lines and speaking consolation with my fingers.

'They have found James,' she says, and it is the first time that his name has been spoken here for longer than I can remember. Even when he was here we did not use his name. The men playing dominoes look away, bury their eyes in the game, but my sister holds my gaze unflinchingly.

I have no words for her. I continue to stroke her temple and she allows her face to go limp, empty even of sorrow, as if she can no longer remember the shapes of grief she wore so achingly vibrant sixteen, nearly seventeen, years ago. There is a struggle visible in her eyes: she wants to show something soft, to throw on the butterfly colours of her youth. But she is frightened, and the fear washes the colours out.

In the doorway behind her, I see Claire, wearing in all its newness the brightness of youth that has faded upon her mother, but her look of curiosity betrays no hint of comprehension.

And in the woods beyond the fields lies James's body, not far from the spot where I found him more than seventeen years ago, waiting for the men to bring him in again.

All things buried come to the surface eventually and so too must this.

August, 1914

The sun was shining the day the Germans took our village, the day they marched into the square with their pointed helmets gleaming, dragging heavy canons, pulled by horses. The sun was shining as they lowered the *tricolore* flag that flew above the *mairie*: red and white and blue cloth bathed in yellow sunlight. The sun was shining the day they came, although there was blood scattered, red as the poppies in the cornfields.

The summer of 1914 was yellow with the sun and the ripened corn. I remember my father lifting me high on his shoulders above the fields, turning me round and round so that blue sky and gilded corn and red poppies ran together in dizzying strands.

It was a summer filled with noise and colour, as the great cavalcade of war descended upon the countryside of Northern France. I remember the bright uniforms of the French soldiers who marched eastwards down the lanes. I remember the smiling faces of the British Tommies who came after them, their songs of victory fading in the hedgerows. We gave them lemonade, bread, posies of flowers from the fields as they marched off to war. I remember that the corn ripened in the fields and the sky was a flat, vast blue and we heard talk everywhere, talk red as the poppies on the outskirts of my silence: talk of a German army advancing through Belgium, burning the villages as they came; talk of scorched cornfields and villages on the run.

Then came the refugees, fleeing from Belgium, pushing their belongings in carts or prams, through our village. I heard their tales of a German army, bigger than any armed force Europe had ever seen, of their homes ransacked, their cities in flames.

And then in August the retreat. The French and the English rolled back again, their units disbanded. They were wounded, many of them, lost and broken in retreat and I could see fear in their eyes. In their wake, they left packs, greatcoats, canteens, which we children found scattered in the hedgerows. They abandoned their belongings as they ran and left behind their wounded. And afterwards we would learn that many lost their units and had no choice but to run, uncertain of the direction. Some ran to the woods and others in the direction of Cambrai, east, not west, back into the advancing phalanx of the enemy.

Some people from our village packed their

belongings hastily and joined the crush of people fleeing westwards on the roads. Those of us who remained hid our valuables beneath floorboards, in back gardens, sheds and barns. For, close on the heels of the retreating French and British armies, we heard the sound of German guns and shells exploding.

★　★　★

The sun was shining the day the Germans took the village. I saw it all from the woods. I had gone out early to collect mushrooms and I saw it all take place in the fields below, terrified, stiff with fear, the forgotten mushrooms scattered in the dirt.

A handful of British soldiers clung on to the ridge above the village until midday, firing wildly, covering the hasty withdrawal of their colleagues, before they too retreated. Then I saw the German horsemen gallop through the corn with lowered lances to flush out any remaining soldiers who might be hiding there.

I watched as the ranks of grey filed through the village, heard the shouts as men were ordered out of the houses, into the streets, gunshots fired as warnings into the air.

I stayed where I was all day, hidden among

the darkening trunks until I saw the sun lower over the ridge. The sunset was oddly pungent that evening, filled with the smell of fires as the German troops set up camp. My limbs were aching with the effort of remaining still, the mushrooms I had abandoned long since and I was cold now, as the slow cool trickled across the fields. It was nearly evening when I started back.

I made my way along the edge of the fields, where the corn was ablaze with the sunset, the meadow flowers closing their heads against the dying of the light. There was spring barley in this field and, late in the year as it was, it had not yet been harvested for so many of the village men had gone off to fight, leaving the harvest to those women and older men who remained. The corn was nearly as tall as I was and I crouched among the stalks, hidden in the rows as I made my way towards the village.

Suddenly a guttural shout cut across the brazen air. I crouched quickly, curling myself to nothing among the stalks, my breathing quick, frightened. My foot was caught in a small drainage ditch, lodged against something solid, unable to move, and I felt a sharp pain shoot up my ankle.

The voices receded and my breathing slowed. I adjusted myself to get my foot free and as I did so I saw a hand, rising like a withered stump from the earth. Through the stalks the rest of the body was visible, bathed in evening light like a gentle shroud, coating the brown-green uniform and crystallizing the face so that it seemed mummified: blue dead flesh tinged with gold. There was no sign of a wound, but the water at the base of the ditch was red in colour, life blood growing stagnant as the corn grew up out of it. I stared at the dead soldier for some time, transfixed by the blue eyes that seemed alive and the delicate patterns that death had traced on the young man's skin.

I tugged my foot free and scrambled through the stalks, towards the copse now, the last bit of cover before the village.

The light was declining, a hazy yellow orb visible on the horizon, from where sounds of gunfire now came, shattering the ripe stillness in the fields, one side blasting at the other in a desperate evening offensive.

I slowed down once I reached the copse. Amongst the trees it was almost dark, only thin strips of orange light visible between the charcoal barks. There was ivy to muffle the sound of my feet, and beneath them the recollection of the spring flowers underfoot, snowdrops and crocuses, trapped beneath the soil like memory or unspoken words, sleeping out the remains of the year before the distant spring of their blooming.

The previous spring we had been there, my sister and I, gathering snowdrops, the light falling like white blossom on our skin. Now the evening fell, muffling sound so that the rustling my feet made was muted, distant, cocooned.

I felt his hand before I heard anything. Felt the rough, chapped skin pressed against my face, my body roughly pulled back. I screamed. His hand had not clamped securely enough and sound escaped through his muddy grip, my desperate exhalation startling us both and setting up a flurry of movement within the tree tops.

I could hear him breathing behind me, hard, as if he had been running and yet I had not heard him approach. He smelt of sweat and earth and something bitter, like the scent of a dead creature rotting in the hedgerow. My heart-beat was a frantic pulse beneath his low animal breaths but I stopped struggling. Gradually his grip relaxed and I felt him falter.

'Quiet! Quiet! I won't hurt you.' The French he used was unfamiliar somehow. The accent was bastardized and it had a different lilt to it, discernible even in its whispered urgency.

Still holding me, he staggered backwards, against a tree trunk. He was panting. I could feel the agony of his quick breaths against my ear, his grip on me loosening. The orange sky bloomed defiant behind the blackening tree trunks.

'If I let you go, will you be quiet?' he asked, his breaths slowing a little, but still shallow.

I offered my silence up to him with a nod and he loosened his grip with a gasp, allowing his body to fall back against the trunk. It was then that I saw one of his legs had been shot to pieces and hung out, limp and blood-crusted in front of him as his face winced with pain.

There was blood on my dress, where his hand had pressed against my skin and I lifted my arm to brush it off with my sleeve, without taking my eyes off the slumped figure in front of me.

The uniform he wore I recognized as British, although I did not know the insignia of his regiment. He was young, maybe mid-twenties, but the skin about his face was loose, slack, as if he had too much to cover his angular features. It was his eyes that gave the appearance of youth: grey-brown, they were light in the darkness, reflecting my own white face in them.

'Did I hurt you?' he asked.

I did not move.

'I'm sorry if I frightened you.' He was still breathing heavily, scarcely able to concentrate on my response, unaware that I had said nothing.

'The Germans are here?' he asked, looking east in the direction of the gunfire. I nodded and his head fell back against the trunk, an expression of frustration and pain flicking across his face. Then his eyes came back to me. He let out a short, pained laugh. 'I'm trapped.'

He smiled as he said it, as if it was a joke. For a moment I did not read the wryness in his expression and I surprised myself by smiling back. That made him laugh once more.

'Well, I can't think of any one nicer to be trapped with than you,' he said, using the adult form of the pronoun so that the expression sounded old-fashioned, formal, and I was not sure if he was mocking me. Then, 'I need you to help me,' he said.

Fear breathed through me as a small, sharp breeze disturbed the treetops and sent up a flurry of movement. I looked at his leg, at the wound which was already clouded with grey, like the sheen that appears on meat when it is a few days old, and I looked at his face. It was not so different from that of the dead soldier in the ditch. The grey had not advanced so far, but his eyelids glowed white in the darkness and I knew that if he stayed out there all night, the next day I would find him stiff as the body in the ditch, slumped against the tree, his grey eyes flat and open.

I pulled away quickly, frightened now, but he grasped my arm, wincing with the effort.

'I need food' he said. I tried to tug away from his grip, but it was firm and I could not get free. Already the blood was drying on my dress and I could smell it upon my face, crusting around my mouth. I thought of the blood of the dead soldier stagnating in the ditch. I did not pull away.

In my apron I had a piece of bread, uneaten from earlier in the day. I pulled it out, warm and flattened, and he took it and ate ravenously, speaking only between mouthfuls to express his thanks.

I stood watching as he gasped with the relief of swallowing, his Adam's apple pulsing in his throat. When he had finished he reached a limp hand into his jacket and pulled out a cigarette-case, silver. Even in the grey light it glowed, its contours smooth as a pebble, except where initials had been etched on it along with an inscription. His hand lingered over it before he flicked it open and pulled out a cigarette. He seemed almost unaware of my presence and I was invisible for a moment as he took a match and cupped his hand carefully as he struggled to strike it. A sudden brief illumination of orange, the sharp tang of tobacco smoke, and his face bright suddenly, lit eerily from below, then a low sigh as he extinguished the match hastily and we were in darkness again, only the red tip of the cigarette, like a regal glow-worm in the night. He inhaled, looked at me, released a cloud of white into the gloaming.

'Thank you,' he said.

I watched him. He sucked on the cigarette, pulled it out from between his lips, offered it to me.

'Want some?' he asked, smiling.

I shook my head, though the imagined taste nagged at my tongue. I wanted to step forward, suck in the thick pungent smoke, but I did not.

'What's your name?' he asked.

I shrugged, kept my eyes on him.

'I'm James,' he said. 'You?' And something stirred in me, as if that which blocked my throat shifted just for a moment. And I half-opened my lips to whisper a reply, then it settled back into place and the words were trapped again.

'You should go,' he said after a moment.

I remained still, more cocooned than ever by my silence.

'Go on. Go home.'

I hesitated.

'Your mother will be worrying,' he said and an image of my mother rose in my mind, unbidden, a memory of her I did not know I had kept — of her sitting on the steps in front of the café, laughing. A faint scent of poppies lifted in the night air. I turned to go.

'Thanks for the bread.'

I turned back.

'Shake hands?' He balanced the cigarette between his lips and offered me his right hand. I hesitated for a moment before stepping forward, gingerly, offering my own. It was a gesture I was not familiar with, intimate in its formality. He took my hand, held my eye.

'Thank you,' he said, shaking vigorously, a smile playing on his lips, the lit orange end of the cigarette glowing between them. He let go, took the cigarette out and exhaled, a cloud of smoke cloaking him, white in the darkness.

I moved off, quickly now. It was night already beneath the trees. Grey strips of cloud overlaid the blue and the moon was visible already. There were roots, hidden beneath the cloak of the leaves and low branches to confound my way and I tripped often, suddenly afraid in the darkness. I did not look behind me, but all the way home I could hear the hiss of his indrawn breaths, low and shuddering below the night breeze and in my nostrils a scent remained, of blood and tobacco and poppies.

When I got back to the house, the Germans were there.

★ ★ ★

I remember the British and French soldiers who had been taken prisoner, huddled around the fountain in the village square. I saw what they did to them that night as I slipped back through the village.

There were three soldiers, one French, two British, all three wounded, eyes downcast, uniforms of thick serge heavy upon them. The green of the British uniforms was muddied out in the clammy night air, their white faces glowing in the dark. There was one with flame-red hair. Beneath his cap, it was orange, like a fox's and he stared forward, not at us, but beyond to the bruised fields, where his comrades marched their long retreat from Mons towards the River Marne.

I remember the short, fat orstkommandant who barked instructions and the long moment of anticipation as the firing-squad pulled their triggers. I remember the bullets piercing furrows in the luminous air, following their tracks with my eyes and seeing each one make an impact with chest, flesh, uniform. A moment of entry then a flowering. Blood blooming at their chests as the figures convulsed, pulled taut then, suddenly limp, fell heavy and disordered on the stone steps, skulls crashing on stone, body on body, contorted.

The red-haired soldier was still breathing. That is what I remember most of all. He was gasping, his hands flailing like a desperate swimmer. Blood spilled from his mouth, and he screamed, high and long, like a child. Then another bullet stilled his writhing, a shot punctuated by a final cry and then silence, the night air still, but for the bullet smoke and the cloudy white of my breathing, suddenly visible as I panted like fear.

The orstkommandant turned to bark at the firing-squad. I remember the sound of his voice as I watched the blood of the young boys trickling between the cobbles, running scarlet, just as the poppies had run in scarlet threads when my father turned me round and round in the yellow fields.

They made the mayor watch, and the *curé*, standing on the white cobbles, bathed in moonlight, to observe the ritual. Afterwards they marched them off, the *curé*, an old man in black robes stumbling in the darkness. The orstkommandant shouted instructions, muddying the dark night with thick-lipped consonants.

And I stood watching, the memory of the other British soldier, the one in the woods, rasping like dog breaths through my head.

★   ★   ★

When I reached the yard at the back of our house, I could hear German voices from within.

My stomach lurched. There was blood on my dress, blood of an Englishman staining the air around me with its stench. I forced myself into the shadows, night cloaking my face but not the hot scent of blood and fear. I listened, my heart beating high in my chest.

Someone was speaking in French, well-turned vowels, polluted by German gutturals. I did not hear what he was saying, my heart pounding in my ears.

The door on to the yard was open and, from my vantage point I could see my sister moving in and out of the larder, laying things on the table, while my father stood, still, silent, his face set, fists clenched. A soldier stood by the larder door, watching my sister move, eyes moulding over her contours as I have seen other men's do. A second soldier shouted from below and then emerged through the cellar door with a crate of wine. He banged it on the table and shouted something.

The third man, the one whom I could not see, the one who had spoken in French, seemed to rebuke him in their own language.

I saw my father look up, surprised. The third man, evidently the superior officer, delivered a curt order and the soldier twitched to attention.

'Leutnant Voller', he barked, then I saw him pick up the crate of wine and return it to the cellar. I saw too the quick glance of frustration he darted at his comrade before he disappeared.

'You will open the café as normal tomorrow,' Leutnant Voller was saying to my father, speaking in French again. 'You will serve my men but they must pay for what they drink.'

He moved now towards the door and I could see him, half-silhouetted in the dim gaslight.

He had white-blond hair, the colour of buttermilk. His face was ruddy, and he was tall, taller than the soldier in the woods, but about the same age.

My sister moved to let him pass and he nodded in her direction but she did not raise her eyes to meet his. He moved quickly and I shrank back from the doorway.

I pressed hard against the wall, trying to hide the side that had the bloodstains, consign it to the shadows. But his eye was caught by my white dress, glowing in the light which spilled from the doorway. He stopped, just under the lintel, looked at me.

I was breathing hard, and I could almost hear James's low breaths panting beneath my own. Blood rushed to my cheeks, warm, and red as the blood that had stained my skirt. He surveyed my face, then turned back to the figure of my sister, still visible beside the fire. I saw that his eyelashes too were white-blond, translucent in this light.

He looked at me, then back at Thérèse. 'Sisters,' he said, almost beneath his breath. Then he nodded and moved away.

I remained motionless, cold fingers of the night making me shiver as I watched his retreating form, sharp footsteps ringing high on the cloudless night, audible, long after he had gone. Tick, tick, tick, tick.

February, 1932

The British cemetery lies just outside the village. It is visible from the road, lying in a slight dip between two fields. The light catches the incline oddly so that in the field that rises above it the chalky furrows are illuminated in uneven strips, while the field below lies in shadow. In the summer the corn in the two fields grows different hues, as if the cemetery were still a kind of no man's land, battle lines marked out in shades of gold.

The cemetery itself is rectangular, with a low stone wall enclosing the rows of white headstones. Identical, they stand, row on row, the same inscription on many: A soldier of the Great War: Known unto God. This seems to offer more comfort than the bald word on the French crosses: *Inconnu*, Unknown. The British dead are known unto someone, it seems, even if it is only a god in whom so many of them lost their faith.

The grass is kept neat and each grave is tended. Spring flowers grow here and there, between the headstones, so that when the evening light falls the effect is of glowing rows of white, casting long black shadows on the grass alongside brilliant files of colour: blues and yellows, crimson-dipped in the failing light. And framing the cemetery in high summer the corn grows, waving its indifference on golden stalks, smelling of seed-time and harvest, a golden testimony that the earth's yearly round still spins about this square of stillness.

It is raining today, a light spring drizzle which blanches all colour out of the sky. The ground is wet underfoot and our shoes are quickly damp and grass-stained, the cold seeping through uncomfortably.

We make our way, the three of us, my sister, Claire and I, to the small plot on the far side where the ground is freshly dug and where a small collection of people has gathered. We see them from across the field: two of them are dressed in black, while the other, a woman, stands a little further apart, wearing everyday clothes. As we draw closer, I recognize the new *curé*, talking to the two in black. The other woman has turned away, looking out across the fields, her hands crossed in front of her, and although I have not seen her in over sixteen years, I recognize her immediately.

My sister has also noticed her and her steps falter a little. The woman is alone, shivering in damp clothes. I wonder how long she has been here. I look away as she turns in our direction, not wanting to meet her eye.

The pair in black are together: a young man, tall, just on the brink of manhood. He does not lift his head and so I cannot see the colour of his eyes, but for all that, I know who he is. Next to him stands a woman of about forty, dark-haired, features hidden at this angle by the brim of her hat. She looks oddly out of place here in the fields.

At my side, I am aware of my sister's taut stillness. Beside her, Claire shivers a little in the cold. She does not know who they are and this ignorance makes her seem suddenly fragile. They stand together, mother and daughter, child taller than the parent, like a mirror image of the couple on the other side of the cemetery.

A few other people have come now and the ceremony has started, so we stay back, at a distance, listening to the words that the *curé* scatters over the empty earth. He speaks in English, a murmured prayer and the woman in black bows her head. The young man does not join in the prayer, and I wonder if the all-knowing God to whom the gravestones refer is one that is unknown to him. He looks about him, taking in the cemetery, the blank sky, the three of us stood at a distance. His eyes light on Claire and linger there for a moment. Perhaps he sees the same thing in her features that I do in his, for his eyes flicker back to her twice more while the *curé* intones his liturgy.

The *curé* speaks in French now, using the language of honour and sacrifice which blows idly about and falls damp to the earth in the spring drizzle. He speaks of loved ones bereft, left behind to mourn, speaks of the pain of not knowing, the need to lay our dead to rest.

I feel my sister tense beside me and I reach out a tentative hand to take hers. Through the soft calfskin glove I can feel her hand trembling. Her body remains unwaveringly still, her face set, only the breeze disturbing a strand of milk-blonde hair at her temple. The woman in black looks up and her eyes meet my sister's for an instant before she quickly lowers them.

She is dark-haired, well-dressed, a little older than my sister. Her skin looks tired and I wonder if the hair is dyed. Her son stands at her side, her hand in both of his. The light is behind them, their features indistinct, faces merely pale triangles as the young lad from Cambrai plays the last post, falteringly, the high notes rising uncertainly through the damp air.

There is silence now as the box is lowered into the ground. We all stand and watch as the earth is rained down on the space where my soldier now lies: the two women, one on either side of his grave, one blonde, one dark; and the young man with grey-brown eyes who stares at Claire as the final notes die across the fields.

By the time winter of 1914 had set in, you could see the scar of the trench line from where we are standing. When the wind was easterly you could hear the sound of the guns as if they were no more than a hundred yards away, and James said that on such days, when he was alone, he fancied he could hear the screams of the soldiers caught in their fire. I think it held a fascination for him, he could think of little else as he hid, and I suspect that he would rather have laid down his body in the fields six miles west of here than for his last resting place to be in the quarry, so far east of the front line.

The service is over now. We watch as the *curé* talks to the woman and her son, watch the way his mouth opens and closes, words inaudible, dumb as a fish. The young man is holding his mother's hand again, close to his chest, clasping it in both of his, and I notice for the first time that this hand is bare, although on the other she wears a glove.

I turn to Thérèse who remains totally still at my side. I do not expect her to go to them but she does. Perhaps it is curiosity that impels her across the muddy grass to where they stand, the pair in black.

She steps up to the young man first and for a moment, it is as if the two of them stand face to face again. She holds his gaze for a fraction longer than is polite, then moves on to the woman at his side.

The woman's eyes meet those of my sister. The two women stand face to face and my sister says, 'We are sorry for your loss.'

And she says it almost absently, so that I do not know if this is real or words she has polished, smooth as pebbles over the years, slowly stroking them to herself, unspoken, silent. And I wonder, not for the first time, if she knew all along.

Then she steps away, gives no hint of what she is thinking, hugging herself against the cold, her slim figure girlishly elegant, her stockinged legs splattered with mud. Claire follows her, a little behind, taller although the shoes she wears are lower. The woman turns away, unaware it seems, but the young man watches them go.

They have not noticed me, but I step up and take his hand now. For a second I hold it, and he says, 'Thank you very much for coming.' Accent oddly faltering. All I can do is nod a response. I turn to the woman at his side, take her hand, the ungloved one, which her son has now released. Her skin is cold in the damp spring morning and I want to stroke it, but I do not. I hesitate for a moment then release her hand and turn to go. I can hear the young man say something to the curé, but I do not turn back.

Magali Legrange is waiting in the path, just outside the gate. She is thinner now than I remember her and even from a distance I can see that her features, always plainer than my sister's, have been slashed with shadows. I feel a momentary impulse to run over and greet her, to pretend nothing has happened. She still has the same soft smile, gently curving at the corners, briefly illuminating the blue eyes. Her grey coat, beautifully cut, has grown too big for her and her hands look white and fleshless, clutching a bag.

'Hello, Thérèse,' she says, simply.

She looks tired. I have heard that her father is unwell. He has not recovered from the war, they say, from the time he spent in the prison camp in Frankfurt. She nurses him now, in the house they moved to in Peronne. She has come a long way today.

Her greeting hangs limp in the damp air.

She looks as if she does not expect a response and my sister gives her none. She meets Magali Legrange's eye briefly as she

31

passes, but that is all. If I had anticipated drama, I am disappointed. Magali turns away.

Then she catches sight of me and a flicker of belated recognition crosses her face. I am no longer the child that she remembers, but a woman now, taller than she.

'Hello,' she says, raising one hand, the other holding on to the little bag. Her hand is blue with the cold but the curve it makes is smooth, moulding the damp air into a greeting.

I stand for a moment, the drizzle between us, words, unspoken in years rising to my throat where they remain, stuck. My tongue lacks eloquence to say what I want to and so I simply nod and turn away.

And so now we are all assembled. Myself and Magali Legrange the last two needed to complete the drama. Looking back, I see the young man reach in his pocket, take out a silver cigarette case and turn it about in his fingers.

August, 1914

My sister was ten when my mother died. Old enough to feel the loss in ways I did not. My grief crystallized into silence while hers broke away in shards. My silence was white, opaque, toneless rendering me invisible, but the colours of her anger were bright, regal colours: scarlets, purples and golds surrounding her in radiance, like reflections from coloured glass and she, in the centre, was stained by them, as if caught in the rays from a bright church window. She was strong and brittle in equal measure, and her defiance made her look lost sometimes, fragile, breakable. She could be angry, but her anger overreached itself, tumbling, like a great wave, collapsing, as if she did not know what she was angry at.

★　★　★

It was late. After ten o'clock; a couple of hours since I had found the soldier in the woods. Normally we would have been in bed, but the noise of the German troops outside, banging on doors, shouting commands, meant that we could not rest, but sat in silence, listening to the sounds of occupation. I watched my sister. She attempted to sew, but her needle hovered over the cloth, still for seconds at a time, before stabbing almost aimlessly at the fabric. Her movements were restrained, but sitting at her feet I could hear the short, low exhalations of breath each time the fabric puckered and I could see the restlessness in her fingers.

There was a loud rap at the door. None of us moved. I saw my father glance at my sister, then stand. He walked towards the door, his movements deliberate, uncertain.

A man was standing in the darkness and it took a moment for my father's eyes to adjust to his features and to take in the details of his uniform: the colour, the boots, heavier than German boots, thick roan leather, British army standard issue. Before he had said anything the man collapsed forward and my father caught him. We were all on our feet in a scraping of chairs, and my sister's needlework fell disordered to the floor.

It was my sister he saw as he staggered. Her face must have been the one that he lifted his eyes to as my father steadied him. But I did not see the expression on his face, for I was watching Thérèse.

My father was dragging him in and

hushing us all, supporting the stranger on his shoulder until he got him into a chair. Then he turned hastily to close the door, looking about outside anxiously before he did so. And it was then that I saw it was my soldier.

'Nobody saw me,' the man gasped and I could tell that my father was surprised to hear him speaking in what was audibly French although his voice rasped with pain.

He caught his breath before lifting his head and, as he did so, the wound on his thigh became bloodily visible and my sister inhaled quickly at the sight of it. For it was worse now, yellow pus seeping from it. He looked up and saw me staring at him.

He had not noticed me until now and as his gaze met mine, I saw surprise registered there, quickly replaced by a light that looked like laughter. But he did not say anything. He smiled at me, fleeting, brief, as if at a shared joke, then turned back to my father.

'I'm sorry,' he said. 'I don't mean to bring trouble on you.'

My father still said nothing. A beat pulsed the air. Then, 'You must be hungry.'

James nodded, relief flooding his face.

My sister tended to his wound while I prepared food. She used scissors to cut the fabric away and I saw how his face contorted with silent agony as she worked. My father gave him a glass of Blanche, the white local liqueur that stings the throat and dulls the pain, and soon his breathing slowed and he answered my father's questions.

I sliced the knife through bread, my eyes averted, unable to look but aware of my sister's scissors making contact with his flesh.

'How long have you been out there?' my father asked.

'Three days.' A sharp intake of breath.

'What happened to you?'

'We were part of the retreat from Mons. Bringing up radio equipment. We had a field wireless and spare accumulators. We were trying to get them back to brigade HQ. I took a bullet in the leg. German sniper. Saw me before I saw him. Took out three of my men. Ah!' He winced and my knife faltered, sensible of the soft texture of the bread beneath the blade. 'I told the others to go on, leave the equipment. I covered their retreat then followed, but I couldn't get far on this leg. Ah!' He winced again.

'He needs a doctor,' my sister said, her voice low, not meeting the British man's eye.

'Oh, God!' He expelled the sound like an unwanted breath, muttering in English for a moment, then: 'I'm sorry.' My father said nothing and my knife was still. 'I don't wish to place your family in danger,' he said, but there was an appeal in it.

My father remained silent and it was my sister who said:

'I could get Doctor Legrange.'

None of us said anything.

My father broke the stillness with movement. He reached for his coat and made for the door.

'I'll get Legrange,' he said. 'Feed him.' And he went out into the night, leaving us alone with my soldier whose leg was bleeding afresh, soaking the clothes blood-red.

He sat, unspeaking, while my sister ladled out soup into a bowl. I smeared butter over the thick slices of bread.

'You are very kind,' he said, as I gave him the bread. I reddened and moved away quickly.

My sister darted me a look, said nothing. Then she asked him his name, the question curt, clipped.

'James. Captain James Winter,' he said, and the name rested in the air and I felt as if I had heard it before. 'And you?' This to my sister.

'Thérèse.'

He repeated the name. Smiled. 'It's a nice name.'

'And you?' He looked at me and I turned away, confused by his gaze.

'She doesn't speak,' said my sister. She

handed him the bowl of soup, but his eyes remained on me for a moment, quizzical.

Then he ate, not as he had earlier, but more slowly now, as if it hurt to swallow. And my sister remained standing in the corner, holding the cloth in front of her, the light from the oil-lamp and the fire casting yellow shadows on her. We both watched him as he ate in silence, waiting for my father to return.

★   ★   ★

Doctor Legrange used scissors to remove the fabric that had become stuck into the wound and James's face contorted with silent pain as he worked. I watched, did not take my eyes off the flat silver blades as they probed into the flesh, cut away fabric and dropped it bloody into a bowl on the floor.

The doctor asked questions, but he seemed to do so more to occupy James than out of any interest in the replies, for he did not appear to listen.

'Where's your regiment?' he asked.

'I don't know.' James breathed in sharply and I could tell that he was trying to contain a cry. 'The order to retreat reached us late. We had to move the radio equipment to the new Brigade headquarters. Ten of us. It was slow going; we were an easy target. I lost three of my men. Took a hit myself. I . . . ' he broke off.

'Where?'

'East of here, I think. Near a quarry.'

'How long ago?'

'Three days,' James replied.

'Where did you learn to speak French?'

'At school,' he said. 'Charterhouse. I learned French and German,' he added and as he did so he gasped. The pain was such that he could not talk any more and his head rolled back and he reached out for something to hold.

It was my sister who offered her hand and he grasped at it. His eyes were closed and he seemed unconscious of her presence or of anything but the agony that had consumed him.

I watched the way that his hand grasped hers, the same hand that had shaken mine earlier, noted the whiteness about his knuckles. The doctor was using a heated knife now and each time he probed in the wound I watched James's hand tighten over my sister's so that it almost seemed as if he would crush it. Between each motion he relaxed a little, opening his eyes slightly, pupils oddly dilated, unseeing. My sister took a cold cloth and pressed it against his forehead which was beaded with sweat. His eyes were fixed as her face leant close to his, his breath heavy and his pupils tightly focused and yet they seemed not to see her.

When Doctor Legrange had finished he cleaned the wound and bound it with strips ripped from an old towel. Slowly James's breathing steadied and the wooden rigidity in his limbs loosened to a trembling. He allowed my sister's hand to drop, but not before becoming dimly aware that he had been clasping it. He turned to her in apology, but she looked away, not allowing their eyes to meet again.

'I'm sorry', he said. 'Did I hurt you?'

She rubbed her hands in her apron and shrugged, the motion self-conscious. His eyes remained on her for a moment longer before turning to Doctor Legrange.

'Thank you,' he said. 'Thank you very much.'

My father had been seated throughout. He did not have his usual prop of his pipe with him and his fingers seemed redundant, sitting oddly square on the table, drumming nervously. Now he rose, and said:

'You can stay tonight. Tomorrow you will have to go.'

★   ★   ★

James slept in my bed that night and I slept in my sister's room. She remained downstairs late into the night with my father and Doctor Legrange, talking. I lay awake, listening to the conversation, caught in snatches.

'We can't. What will he do.' This was my sister's voice, soft and urgent.

The men's voices were lower, harder to fathom in the humid night air, thick with summer's wine. ' . . . put us all in danger,' were the words I caught. Then. ' . . . wound needs tending to . . . he'll get a fever.' And again something from my father that I did not catch, then my sister: 'You saw what they did.' And I knew that she was thinking of the three soldiers in the square, the one with red hair screaming like an animal until they shot him through the head. For they had witnessed the scene from the upstairs window which overlooked the square. My father's response was inaudible.

Something creaked, like the loosening of a floorboard and there was silence below, silence through which fear breathed. I counted in my head all the numbers up to thirty before I was convinced that it was just the old house moving, shifting in its sleep. The conversation below resumed at a whisper and I could hear nothing but a faint sibilance. I must have fallen asleep then for my dreams were full of deep, creeping wounds and an indistinct but pungent smell of fear mixed with whispers and the scent of rotting flesh. I woke often, thinking I had heard the sound of approaching feet outside, or a knock at the door, but all was quiet, save the rasping of James's breathing in the next room as he slept through pain.

Before dawn I woke to hear movement below. I heard the latch lifting, voices in the kitchen: male, the words indiscernible. I manoeuvred myself so that I was sitting up and able to look out of the window, moving cautiously, so as not to wake my sister. The clock on the mantelpiece indicated that it was four thirty as I heard the latch lift again and the sound of feet in the gravel below.

It was still dark and the moon was full, with no clouds and I could see the lane behind the house and the fields beyond that, illuminated blue. In the distance, to the west, there were fires burning and smoke rose in the night air.

I could not see them at first, but as they moved out of the shadows, I could make out three figures. Two of them I recognized: my father, James. The third I did not know. It was not the doctor. They moved out into the lane in slow, deliberate movements, one man on either side of James, supporting his weight as best they could.

Beside me, my sister stirred in her sleep, damp sheets caught around her limbs. The third figure was shorter than my father or James, his gait heavy beneath the weight of the injured man. He turned suddenly, looked back at the house as if he had heard something. In the moonlight, I could just make out his face.

I recognised Henri Marcel instantly.

April, 1932

I am the only one working in the café the day that he comes. It is market day in the nearby town of Cambrai and the village has emptied. Only a few old men sit playing dominoes in the far corner of the café, drawing on pipes, muttering in low tones.

It is raining outside and the café is dark, apart from the orange glow of the gas-lamps. The bottles on the shelves are deep reds, blues and greens, which catch in the flickering light, casting faint glowing reflections on to the floor and the wall.

I see him standing in the road before he comes in. He is smartly dressed in a suit, overcoat and hat, but he is soaking wet. He has brought no umbrella and his clothes are patched dark with rain. He appears to have been walking around for a long time before seeking shelter in the café.

The little bell above the door sounds gently as he comes in and the men look up from their dominoes briefly before lowering their eyes again to the black-and-white ivory oblongs.

He takes his hat off. He has the same

hairline, same slope of the brow. I watch as he removes his overcoat and hangs it on the stand by the door, his back to me now. Then he comes over to the bar. It is gloomy but his wet hair and skin glisten where the rain still clings to them and his eyes catch the rainbow lights from the bottles, red, blue and amber flecks in the grey.

'Good morning,' he says. And the two words are oddly inflected, ringing with foreignness.

I nod.

'Can I have a coffee, please.' He looks about him. 'Do you serve food?'

My eyes dart to the corner and old Jacques speaks without looking up, voice crabbed, phlegmatic. 'She don't speak much. She can get you a bite to eat if you like.'

'Oh.' He looks quickly at me, seems distracted. 'Good, anything you have.'

He is younger than I remembered him. Younger than James was. Only just a man, traces of boyhood still evident in his diffident manner. Men's clothes on a boy's frame.

I know him but he does not know me and the distance between us is hollow but resonant. I have thought before now that there are particles of James woven into me, like stray flakes of his skin meshed into the scar tissue of my memory. They stir now in the presence of this young man with the same eyes, same skin.

He turns away, rubs his hand through his damp hair. As he does so he is reflected in the mirror on the opposite wall, and his double appears in the glass behind the gold and green lettering, framed in gilt. For a moment there are two of him. Mirror images. He looks up and catches sight of his reflection, turns away.

I go out into the back room and cut slabs of cheese and bread for him: the local Marolles cheese with its pungent aroma. Through the open archway, I watch him, sitting down at a table by the window, staring out towards the road where the air is thick with the deluge. He looks tired, caught up in thought. He does not look around him, seems unaware of the men in the corner, the smoke curls that rise to the ceiling and linger there, trapped beneath the cornicing.

I bring out the cheese and bread and some mustard, along with his coffee, and he eats a little, watching the water run in rivulets down the frosted window, washing away the grime that clung to it.

I go back behind the counter, pick up a glass and run a cloth over the smooth, even surface, watch him.

He turns to the men in the corner.

'Excuse me,' he says, and the foreign lilt in his accent is more pronounced now. They look up briefly, appraise him as he speaks, then return their eyes to the game. 'I am trying to find out about someone who was here during the war.'

None of the men looks up, their eyes trained on the game.

'He was a British soldier, in the King's Own Lancaster Regiment. Captain James Winter.' He pronounces the name as James used to: the emphasis on the first syllable, rather than the last in the surname, the short 'i and 'e' that used to sound so odd. 'I wondered if any of you might remember him. If you might be able to help me?'

'Who wants to know?' asks Jacques.

And, although I know already what he will say, I listen as the young man replies:

'I'm his son.' he says. 'Andrew Winter. James Winter was my father.'

The rain is still heavy against the awning and the sound it makes is a low drumming beneath this conversation. In my hand the glass is cold and oily to the touch.

'What do you want to know?' Jacques does not look up. The other man, Piet, the butcher, coughs, hacking phlegm noisily in his throat.

'So he was here, then?'

There is a third man in the café, sitting in

the corner, on his own, smoking and reading the paper. He has not looked up till now. Andrew turns to him.

'Did you know my father?' He asks the question direct.

There is silence now, just the sound of the rain.

Andrew reaches into his jacket pocket and pulls out a wallet. Inside is a photo. He removes it clumsily and pushes back his chair. He walks over to the table where the solitary man sits, puts the picture down in front of him.

'This is my father. Perhaps you remember him?'

The third man, it is Henri Marcel, does not look up. The other two men are resolutely silent. Andrew looks briefly at me.

'He was reported missing in nineteen fourteen. I was six years old.' An image flashes in my mind: a photo of a boy in a sailor-suit, looking shyly at the camera.

No one says anything.

'His body was found near here. At the quarry.' He seems frustrated.

'Please,' he says, taking out a pen and notebook from his pocket. 'Contact me if you are able to tell me any more.' He scribbles a name and address and rips the page out quickly, places it on the table.

He takes a few coins out of his pocket and places them on the bar, looks up at me, nods his appreciation and then pulls on his coat and hat, still damp, and starts out into the rain again.

It is Henri Marcel who speaks. He does not look at me as he does so.

'There was a girl,' he says. Andrew stops, looks back. His hand is on his collar. 'Magali Legrange. She lives in Peronne now. Ask her.'

It is all he says and he does not look up, but keeps his eyes on his paper.

Andrew looks at him. 'Thank you,' he says, aware that silence has enveloped the topic again. A quick glance at me. 'Thank you.' He turns to go.

The bell rings and the door slams, leaving a blast of cold and damp. All is quiet again. I watch him through the glass, standing in the middle of the street, looking left and right, uncertain which way to go.

Henri Marcel does not look up from his pipe when he says: 'I didn't say anything about your sister.'

Jacques laughs, a low throaty gurgling. 'Nor did she.'

I do not look over, but remain where I am, glass in hand, the same one I have been holding the whole time he was here, grown warm now, bearing the prints of my fingers traced on the glass.

★ ★ ★

Later, when the men are gone, I close the café. The rain has stopped now and the wet square is awash with sunshine. I fasten the brass bolt at the top of the door, then walk over to the table where Andrew sat, pick up his unfinished cup of coffee and the half-eaten sandwich. Then I cross to the back, to the tables where the old men were playing dominoes. The little black slabs still lie on the scratched wooden surface, scattered, disorderly.

They have left the scrap from the notebook on which James's son wrote his address. I pick it up, finger it, feeling the stiff yellow and tracing my eyes over the familiar loops of his characteristically English calligraphy, so different from the French.

I recall the other notes: the ones I carried for James, stowed in my apron pocket, away from prying eyes; the final one which I promised to deliver.

I stare at the paper for a moment, then fold it up and put it in my pocket.

★ ★ ★

Sometimes I think it would have been better if he had never come. If he had left me in silence. For I wonder if all he did was to create a new longing in me when he chased away the first. A new emptiness which yawned hollow after he had gone, red raw, like a wound. It has filmed over the years, white scar-tissue stretched transparent over the place where the pain was. But it is still there.

It is quiet in the house. The kitchen has not changed much in seventeen years. There is linoleum on the floor where once there were tiles, and an electric bulb dangles from a fitting in the ceiling. Otherwise there is nothing to tell that time has passed.

I catch sight of myself in the little mirror Claire has placed above the fireplace. For a moment, I do not recognize myself. The sun is oddly luminous in the aftermath of the rain and the shaft from the window catches me at an odd angle, washing out my eyes so they look pale, flat. I run my fingers over my cheek, push a stray strand of hair into place and then turn away. The little square of glass remains on the mantelpiece, impassively reflecting the pattern on the opposite wall, pink roses with grey vertical lines imprisoning them in rows.

Upstairs, I go into the room where I sleep

alone these days. My sister shares with Claire now. Sometimes I miss the dampness of her skin in the morning, the long strands of blonde hair that collected with the dust in corners. Nothing else has changed. On the dressing-table the pitcher and bowl and hairbrush still occupy the same positions. The picture of my mother, a studio portrait taken on her wedding day in which she looks exactly like Thérèse, sits next to the mirror, the enamel frame peeling at the edges now.

I sit on the edge of the bed, open the top drawer of the dressing-table and reach my hand into the back. It is still there, beneath the newspaper lining, the slim cream envelope, a little discoloured with age. I slide it out and look at it. My hands are reflected in the mirror and I watch the way that they turn the little envelope about. The handwriting is the same as Andrew's, the sloping 'W' and assertive strokes on the 't's. It is still unopened. I turn it over, run my fingers over the seal. The glue has dried out and I might easily prise it open. My fingers linger on the corner.

I look up, see myself in the mirror. The sun has gone in and my hair is dishevelled from the morning in the café, my eyes dark. The room behind me is flat on the glassy surface.

I think of the slip of paper in my pocket,

look down at the letter, the addressee's name still visible though the ink has faded, the same name, same address. I turn it once more in my hand, stroke the unbroken seal, then I return it once again to the silent drawer.

August, 1914

Eighty thousand men of the British Expeditionary Force boarded trains at Waterloo in August 1914. I saw their pictures in the paper, smiling as they crossed the channel in troopships, waving to the cheering crowds in Calais, singing as they marched east through French villages. They were on their way to beat back the Kaiser's army, the photo captions said. By the end of that month 20,000 had been killed, wounded, captured or declared missing. This was not reported in the papers, not until the war was over and by then those boys of 1914 were all but forgotten, except by those who had loved them.

The papers hailed the retreat from Mons as a strategic victory, a tactical retreat which held up the German army and put paid to Field Marshal von Schlieffen's plan to topple France in one decisive blow. Only after the war were we to learn that more men had died at Le Cateau than at the battle of Waterloo; and that thousands of those who survived that and the battle of Mons perished during the subsequent retreat. We saw some of these pass through our village. I remember them: their feet bleeding, boots worn quite away, despair in their eyes. Some simply lay down in ditches. Others, injured and separated from their units hid in woods, cellars, hedgerows and barns. Some never saw their commanding officers again. Captain James Winter was just one of thousands whom the British army registered as missing that month.

★　★　★

There was a small brick building in the top field, where my father kept his doves and this was where James was hidden. Dilapidated, half-covered in encroaching ivy from the nearby copse, it was invisible from the village and could be reached by the stream and the wood, where there was cover.

I was sent to take food to him, for it was safer. A child would attract less notice than an adult. And, as my father pointed out, I had no words with which to betray myself.

It was midday and when I first pushed open the door, the bright sun was replaced suddenly by gloom. I could not see for a moment and red spots of light danced before my eyes. There was a smell of musty straw, bird-droppings and damp, and the soft cooing of the doves trilled around me. I did not know what to do, so I just stood there, in the middle of the earth floor, my eyes ranging over the space, waiting for him to move, aware that he was there, somewhere in the stillness, knowing he was watching.

I waited.

A slight rustle made me look quickly to the right but there was nothing there. Then a voice to my left made me jump.

'Cat got your tongue?'

I could make no sense of the words then. Later he would explain them to me; but I recognized his voice and turned round quickly to see him in the shadows, body uneven, slumped over his bad leg, his face less ashen now but ringed with shadows in the gloom.

'Come in,' he said. 'Close the door.'

I turned to do so, stepping briefly into the shaft of sunshine before tugging the wooden door to and shutting out the light. Then it was dark, apart from a few thin slivers of sun that penetrated the old thatched roof and broke up the gloom with long yellow-white threads. I remained by the door, and he beckoned me over to where he stood, in the dark corner.

'Come here.' he said.

I moved slowly, uncertain, my eyes slowly

growing accustomed to the darkness. In the dim light, his features looked unfamiliar. Some of the pain had drained from his eyes and he had washed and shaved so that he looked younger, his skin now tinged with colour. When I got about four feet from him, I stopped, the bundle held in both hands in front of me.

He was breathing heavily, I realized, with the effort of standing on the bad leg and as he reached to take the bundle from me, he faltered a little. I did not release my hold and the fingers of his right hand closed over mine, his one large hand covering my two. I allowed my own grip to loosen, my fingers sliding out from under his and he took the full weight of it.

'Thank you,' he said. I looked down. Although he had washed his body, he still smelt of soap and sweat. He was wearing his mud-encrusted uniform, one trouser leg slashed to the thigh, and the old smell of dried blood was in it. I watched from beneath lowered eyelids as he hobbled back to the corner, behind a pile of scrap timber. There was a shabby blanket thrown on the floor where he had been sleeping.

He found the clothing in the bundle I had handed to him and I saw a flicker of what might have been relief on his face, betraying, for a moment, a glimpse of the fear hidden behind it. Magali Legrange, the doctor's daughter, had brought the clothing round to the café in a bundle this morning. It belonged to her brother, François, who had signed up and marched away three weeks before.

'Turn away,' he commanded. I did not understand him for a moment and remained motionless.

'It's not a peep-show, you avert your eyes, young lady,' he said, fumbling with the buttons of his jacket.

I turned away and I could hear him struggling with his clothing, exhaling breath in pain. I could still see him out of the corner of my eye, pulling on his shirt, his long torso marked with cuts and badly bruised. He twisted a little with the effort of removing the stiff serge jacket and I saw the vertebrae of his spine, descending, one by one, into the small of his back. I had not seen a man naked before, except once, when I was younger, my father, and so through the film of half-closed lashes I watched his slow movements in the dim light, as through a sea.

He was monochrome, the contours of his frame marked in shades of grey. The great wound on his leg was bandaged but the blood had seeped through, and it was dark black now against his slate-grey skin, and he moved cautiously, still in pain. I watched him, hardly daring to breathe.

He turned suddenly, as if aware I was watching. I looked away quickly, embarrassed, not wanting to be caught.

When he had finished dressing, he said, 'You can look now.' I opened my eyes and saw him in colour again. He was taller than François Legrange, but not as broad and the trousers were loose on him. He had removed the British army boots and wore a pair of sabots on his feet and, for a moment in the half-light, he was transformed, as if one of our boys had returned, and the war had never begun.

With some effort he was hiding his own boots and uniform beneath the pile of wood, and not until he had done so did he turn to me.

'OK, now, food,' he said, grinning.

He ate slowly that day, breaking the bread into small pieces, cutting the cheese with a knife, paring the apple and slicing neatly. Not as my father ate, not as I had seen any man eat.

'I heard the guns in the night,' he said, taking a slice of apple and putting it in his mouth. 'Did we hold them, do you know?'

I said nothing.

'I dare say you don't know, even if you

could tell me.' He smiled. 'I don't suppose the Tommies know themselves.' And I liked the way he said the word Tommies, the term I had heard the local men use for the British soldiers. 'Are there more Germans arriving?'

I knew the answer to this, although I could not respond. I was unused to being addressed, asked questions and I reddened, uncomfortable.

'You don't know?' he said, watching me patiently.

It was with an effort that I brought myself to nod.

'There are more troops? Reinforcements?'

I nodded again, awkward still.

'Lots of them?'

I nodded a third time.

'That's not good.'

I thought of hedgerows scattered with packs, greatcoats, rations boxes, sometimes even rifles, all discarded in the hasty withdrawal. We children had looted them for chocolate and tins of bully-beef.

'They think they're going to march through Paris, but we won't let them, will we?' he said, smiling again. I did not know how to respond to this. 'Will you go and fight, do you think?' he asked, face straight, and, although I thought it was a joke, I was not sure, and I felt myself shrink back and my hands tense at my side.

'I'm joking,' he said, grinning again. Then, 'You are a shy one, aren't you.'

I said nothing.

'They say the quiet ones are the best, huh? Not much chance of you giving me away!' I felt as if he was playing with me in some way, laughing at me. 'But I hope you are going to talk to me a bit though,' he said, 'or I shall get lonely.' He spoke as if I were a little child, as others did, but there was a hint of something else in his voice, half-serious.

He sliced off another thin sliver of the apple, balanced it on the knife, held it out to me.

'Here,' he said, 'You want some?'

The knife was caught in a thread of sunlight descending from the ceiling, and the dull silver blade flashed in the sudden illumination. I reached forwards, tentatively took the moist slice of apple from the blade, withdrew and slipped it quickly into my mouth. It tasted sweet, crisp, wet.

'Nice?' he said.

I nodded.

He sliced a bit off for himself, put it in his mouth. I watched him chew and swallow.

'So,' he said, looking at me. 'You never talk?'

Silence, apart from a scratching in the

corner of the barn.

'Don't want to?'

I shrugged. The soft cooing of the doves cushioned the silence.

'That's a shame.' His voice was softer as he said this. 'Can you write?'

I shrug, to tell him: *A little.*

He looked at me, frowning. 'No I suppose not.' He was folding the napkin into neat even triangles, smoothing the edges with long fingers. His hands were hairless, like a woman's, and, although they were cut and scratched and the nails were broken, they did not look like workman's hands. They were smooth, young-looking. My own hands were more gnarled than his.

'Come here,' he said.

I remained motionless.

'I won't hurt you,' he said. 'I want to show you something.'

Still I did not move, although his voice tugged at something in me.

'Come on.' He reached out a hand, the palm turned up towards me, the soft flesh exposed. Slowly, I moved towards it, across the warm earth distance between us, until I was only two feet away.

'Sit down,' he said.

My body was tensed as I sat, my skirt spreading about my thighs. The earth was warm against my calves, prickly with straw.

He reached forward and took one of my hands. I flinched at his touch. He was close now and I could smell the dried blood beneath the clean clothes. He took my hand in his and turned it about. I was conscious that my palms were rough, reddened from work. We were both crouched in the gloom and I waited for him to look at me.

I did not know what he was going to do. He held my right hand cupped in his left so that my palm was upwards and at first I thought he was going to read the lines engrained there, tell me my future, as I had see women do in the market in Cambrai, or at the fête in Arras.

With the fingers of his right hand he was stroking my palm, as if wiping it clean. With his index finger he was making a pattern, tracing it on my palm, the same pattern over and over, becoming clearer each time he did it: an arc, followed by a downwards stroke. He traced it again, looked at me.

'Could you feel that?' he said.

He repeated the sequence. I nodded.

Then his hand loosened its grasp on mine gently and he said: 'Can you do it?'

My eyes darted up quickly to meet his, then down again. I still held his right hand in my left, but my right hand felt awkward now, released from between his long fingers.

'Come on.'

I lifted it slowly, aware of something shifting as I did so, of ice breaking somewhere within me, of a frozen sea shifting. My finger met his palm and the sudden intimacy made me withdraw. He drew my hand back.

'Come on,' he said.

Slowly, my finger traced the arc, watching the lines on his palm.

'Good,' he whispered, his voice soft, his face close to mine as my finger moved into the downward stroke, running the length of the hand until it met the prominent veins in his wrist, and then stopped. I did not draw my finger away, but held it there.

'There,' he said, looking at me, grinning. 'Now you're talking.'

August, 1914

I was not careful on my way back to the café. It was past the curfew that the Germans had imposed and growing dark. All I could think of was the words that my hands had made, the soft impress of his finger on my palm.

I reached the café and pushed the door open, unthinking, stopped short on the threshold. It was full of German soldiers, who turned now to face me: jovial faces, red with beer; blond hair; and grey uniforms. I froze, and blood rushed to my face. One of the soldiers said something and the others laughed, their mirth directed at me. I felt surrounded by it, and I was keenly aware of the contents of the bundle burning in my arms.

I tried to push through them to the bar but one of the soldiers, tall, skinny, with a face like a bird, played a game of trying to stop me, standing in my way so that I had to step round him before he blocked me again. I was hot and I could not look up, aware only of the grey mass of bodies around me, the laughter, the weight of guilt on my arm, panic rising hot. I pushed hard at him and he yielded, laughing, as I reached the bar and ducked through, past my father and back into the house.

In the alcove between the kitchen and bar, where the food was prepared, I stood, breathing hard, eyes stinging. My hands hung limp at my sides and fear choked in my throat, hot tears rising out of my frustration. My father was calling after me, but I did not go back in.

The house stank of laundry, the sickening sweet scent of soap crowded the air. In the kitchen my sister's arms were red and she had tied her hair back with a towel. She was utterly absorbed in the great beast of the activity and did not hear me come in at first. I stood, watching her working, her back straining, surrounded by steam, her hand coming up to her forehead to wipe away the sweat.

She turned and saw me standing there, still holding my bundle.

'You took your time,' she said. 'Come. You can help me.'

I stood for a moment and watched the way her hands worked in the water, grabbing cloth and scrubbing in uneven, jerky movements. Down in the suds they plunged then rose again, dripping and red, kneading the linen like dough. There was a kind of ferocity in the way she worked at times, then a lull and she would stop, hands loose in the water, still for a minute at a time.

'Come on,' she said. 'Don't just stand there staring.'

So, I put down the bundle and rolled up my sleeves. I picked up a pile of linen and took it over to the fire where the iron was warming. There was a kind of pleasure in the searing metal, the burning smell of the linen.

As I worked, I thought of the dim barn, the light in his eyes, the shapes his hands made, the soft touch of his fingers moulding shapes into my skin, sweeping my fingers in clumsy arcs across his palm, releasing trapped sounds into the musty silence.

A sharp rap at the door made us look up.

It was the officer who had been here the previous evening: Leutnant Voller. He stood framed in the back doorway. The room was thick with humidity and the cloying scent of soap.

'Good evening,' he said. My sister looked up, red-faced from the exertion, but she did not return his greeting, pausing only momentarily to wipe away the sweat on her forehead before plunging her hands back into the tub.

'May I come in?' he said.

He removed his hat, placed it under his arm and ducked through the low doorway. He looked around him as he came in, surveying the room, seeing me standing by the fire, then turning back to my sister. She did not stop what she was doing, did not look at him.

'May I?' he said, drawing a chair from the table and sitting on it. He put his hat on the table, sat down so that he was facing where my sister was working. He had a view of her profile, the damp blonde hairs escaping from the ungainly towel she had wrapped over her head.

'My father is in the bar,' she said, not looking at him. The motion of her hands in the water was more jerky now, betraying her self-consciousness.

'Yes,' he said. 'I realize.'

He was younger than I had first thought, possibly younger than James. He was good-looking, although his white lashes accentuated the red rims of fatigue in his eyes and gave his face an albino quality.

'You're busy, I see,' he said, pausing only momentarily for an answer and then moving on. 'I won't stay long.'

He picked up an apple from a bowl of windfalls on the table, rolled it in his hand, passing it palm to palm as he spoke. I watched him, my hands motionless on the iron, feeling the heat seep out of it.

'You have no mother?' he said, awkwardly.

I looked quickly at my sister. She paused mid-motion for a second, almost imperceptibly, before continuing.

'No,' she said. She let the fabric drop back into the tin basin and withdrew her hands, wiping them on a towel.

'She is dead?' Palm to palm he tossed the apple and I noticed that his hands, like James's, were smooth, unused to work. The words too were smooth and polished.

'Scarlet fever.' She put down the towel, uncertain what to do now, moved towards the fire, her back to him.

'I'm sorry.'

My sister did not reply. The door was open, but it was hot and humid within as the steam rose and Voller took out a napkin to mop his glowing brow.

'I lost my sister to scarlet fever,' he said. 'Eighteen months ago.' His words were clipped, the tone formal. 'I can perhaps share your pain.'

'Perhaps.' My sister was brusque as she turned quickly back to the tin basin, tugged out the sheet, dripping on the tiles, and wrung it out, biting her lip with the effort of the exertion.

'Yes. Perhaps.'

He had turned to face her as she twisted the thick material tightly.

He looked over at me. 'You are the sister?' he said.

My sister replied for me. 'Yes, she is.' Vowels tight as the twisted linen.

'Can she not speak for herself.'

In my hand I felt the warm metal of the iron, felt the way it smoothed over the damp linen, like my fingers tracing patterns in James's palm, burning words into it.

'She can't speak.'

'Is she deaf?'

'No.'

'Simple?'

'No.' She answered defiantly for me. 'No, she's not.'

'But she does not speak.'

'She's not spoken for nine years!'

'Has the doctor looked at her?'

'He said there is nothing wrong with her.'

'In Germany such a child would be made to speak or sent away.' He said this quickly, then seemed embarrassed by what he had said. I felt the blood rush to my cheeks, bright red, burning like the linen.

'Maybe.' My sister does not look up. 'In Germany. But not in France.'

He watched her as she dropped the sheet

into a basket on the floor. Steam rose up out of the tub and her face grew redder under his scrutiny.

'Perhaps I can help you with that.' She was picking up the basket of wet linen. He stood, his arms offering to take it for her, but she resisted, crossing the room to the fire, putting down the basket by the clothes'-horse. He followed, standing a few feet away while she hung up the clothes on the wooden horse, watching her.

He still had the apple in his right hand and he ran it between his fingers as he spoke.

'It will be a cold supper tonight, I think?'

She said nothing.

'On a hot day like today. When the laundry has been done. A little bread perhaps, and cheese.'

'We have no cheese. Your men took it.' She turned to him quickly.

'Well, then I shall bring some.' He held her eye for a moment, then turned, picking up his hat. He placed it on his head and his face was in shadow, the blond lashes dark now, casting a curtain over his cheeks, making his sockets appear sunken.

'Please tell your father I have been billeted here.' He tossed the apple back into the bowl, but it missed and rolled off the table, on to the flagstones. I watched it roll under the table. He left it and turned away. 'I will eat supper with your family this evening.'

September, 1914

Leutnant Voller slept in my room, in the same bed that James had slept in. I wondered if he could smell the British soldier in the linen, sense the skin particles of an enemy trapped in the horse-hair mattress or collecting in the dust in the corners.

I shared with my sister who slept deep, caught in the ocean of dreams which tossed her through the night, while mine were in the shallows, just below the surface of waking, often breaking the film, casting me up open-eyed in the blue hours.

Then I would lie and look at her, beside me, limbs tangled in the sheets, moisture around her hair-line, her blonde tendrils damp.

★   ★   ★

Every house in the village had a German soldier billeted with them, some two or even three, and the village spoke in whispers. The town was full of enemy troops and they requisitioned everything, from soap to pots, pans, flour, firewood, mattresses, leather, paper, pigs, hay, straw, corn, carts, harnesses, wine. They took iron to make barbed wire and trees to line the trenches that they were digging west of here. Everything that they could they took, and in return they gave us vouchers, to the value of the goods requisitioned, repayable by the German government four months after the war ended. A family could not eat such vouchers.

For, by early September, the British and German armies had locked over the River Marne. We heard some of this from the soldiers in the café. The British Expeditionary Force had pushed the Germans back as far as the Aisne and then dug in, hastily constructing trenches which would be their homes for the next three years.

But we knew little of this at that time. We knew only that the harvest ripened and turned in the fields and there was no one to bring it in, for all the young men had gone to war. There was a scent of musty decay in the air and the good weather held, but with that bright ferocity which signalled it would soon turn. And so the orstkommandant ordered us out into the fields. Because the young men were away, it was old men, women and children who went.

From seven till noon we worked and from two till six, under the surveillance of

Leutnant Voller's Hussars who beat anyone who hesitated in their work with rifle butts. My sister and I worked in fields close to the village, scarves around our heads to keep off the sun, grubbing for potatoes with our hands in the chalky soil. There was dirt in clods beneath my fingernails, caught in the fine lines of my hands. As far as you could see, only brown earth, stretching to a vast expanse of white sky, the huge pile of potatoes like a glowing white monument on the flat skyline. The crop was turning, we could all feel it, and there were dark clouds massing in the west and so we worked feverishly under the full sun, stopping only briefly to eat black bread wrapped in napkins.

One day, while we stopped to eat lunch, I slipped away. The sun was full overhead. My head was dancing with light-spots, red and purple, and my fingers raw from grubbing in the earth. I knew that I should not risk going now, when someone might see me, follow me, but the heat and the hot clods beneath my feet seemed to impel me. I felt sharp stones sticking into my soles and my head was full of yellow sun as I ducked through the hedgerow and into the copse, running swiftly until I reached the shade and protection of the trees, and then on down the incline to the small brick building where

I knew James was hiding.

It was cool after the heat outside. The smell was different too, earthy, damp. In the corner, the doves cooed, the throbbing sound vibrating in the shaft of sunlight from the open door. Otherwise it was silent, not even the sound of breathing beneath the still air.

I stepped forward. The door squeaked on its hinges.

'Stop there,' I heard a male voice shout from the other side of the barn.

I froze, turned slowly, saw James, revolver in his hand, raised, pointed at me, his bad leg trembling slightly with the weight.

He looked crazed, face set, ready to fire and a pulse of fear throbbed through me.

His face relaxed.

'You!' he half-laughed, and allowed the leg to crumple, staggering back as he let the revolver drop. 'You gave me a fright.'

He turned away, moved back so that he could lean against the wall, catch his breath. I saw him wince and noticed that the blood had already soaked through the fresh bandages my sister had put on his leg.

He looked up. I had not moved.

'Come here,' he said, struggling to sit now, gesturing me to come to him.

Hesitantly, I moved out of the light and over to the corner where he was sitting. I had half-forgotten his face, even in the three days since I had last been to see him, as if I had erased the image by conjuring it too much, and I was startled anew by its clarity.

He was sitting against the wall, leg out straight in front of him. I crouched about a metre away, all thoughts of the fields forgotten, aware only of the silence that surrounded us, of my own breaths and his, my arms hanging redundant at my sides, unable to speak.

'Your hands look battered,' he said.

I looked at them, at the scratches that scarred my palms and the mud encrusted in my cuticles.

'Here,' he said, reaching out, taking my right hand in his. 'Do you want to try again?' He looked at me. I nodded.

His finger found my palm and there was the same ritual of wiping it clean, like a slate on to which words will be drawn. I shifted a little, his touch unfamiliar.

It was a different shape he marked out this time, and I watched his hand as he delineated it, watched the motion of his finger over my palm.

'Hello,' he said, repeating the word as he repeated the gesture.

'Now you try,' he said.

I cupped his long white hand in my brown

one and traced a shape on to his palm, imitating the indentations he made on my own.

'Nearly,' he said. Then he took my hand in his and traced the same pattern with only a slight variation. 'See.'

I watched and copied, mirror image, hands moving like his, intelligible syllables stroking words into warm skin.

'Good,' he said. Then he took my hand again, tracing a new shape. He repeated the gesture. 'How are you?' he said, speaking the words as his hands moved.

Slowly, awkwardly, I attempted to copy it.

'Great,' he said. 'You're good at this.'

I smiled.

'And you've got a smile like your sister.'

I reached into my apron and drew out an apple I had saved. I passed it to him, shyly.

'Is this for me?' he asked. 'Thank you. Is it yours?'

I nodded.

I wanted to ask him how he knew about the gestures, who taught him to speak with his hands, to ask him to show me more words, all the words, but instead I just crouched, watching him eat, waiting for him to show me more.

I did not go back to the fields that afternoon and nobody missed me. I forgot the warm smell of the potatoes, the texture of dirt against my hands, forgot the yellow-and-blue day. In the barn it was brown and dark, damp and cool but the words rose like bubbles from my hands.

The sun declined and even in the barn the quality of the darkness changed, the thin shafts of light fell almost horizontal across the floor, gold, not white and their gilt more shadowy now.

He had stopped using his hands. He was tired and he lay back, head against some sacking while I crouched a little bit away, watching the way his lips formed words that were released in bubbles of sound.

He asked me about where I lived, phrasing his questions so that I could reply in silent negatives and affirmatives. He was grasping for a sense of where he was, asking where the roads led to, about the fields on either side of us. He wanted to know where his comrades were, the distance by which he now lagged behind his army.

'Can you walk there in a day?' he asked.

I shook my head.

'Two days? Three?'

I shrugged.

'From here, can you see the fighting?'

I shook my head.

'From where then?'

I pointed west, to where the sun was starting to decline.

'Can you do something for me?' he asked.

I nodded.

'I need to get to the radio equipment. We had to leave it behind. We left it near an old quarry, not far from here. East, I think.'

I nodded.

'Do you know it?'

I swung my hand round a little, north-east, to the ridge where the old phosphate mine was, where sometimes my father had taken me to fly the battered kite he had made for me. From there you could see down into the whole valley, as far as Cambrai on a clear day, and over to Arras in the west.

'Can you draw for me?' he asked, fumbling in his pockets for a stump of pencil and something to write on. His movements were awkward still, the dead leg in front of him making him grunt as he twisted his body.

He had no paper, so he pulled out a photo he had kept in his pocket and passed it to me. It was a picture of a little boy, about six years old, dressed in a sailor-suit and staring at the camera. A painted backdrop depicted a forest and the child looked oddly ill at ease in this setting.

James turned the photo over and passed me the stub of a pencil.

'Can you draw for me, where the quarry is from here?' he asked.

I looked at the yellowing reverse of the photo, which was blank except for a date: 'July, 1914.' And initials: 'A.W.'

Then I picked up the pencil and drew faint lines on the card, sketching the quarry as a crude rectangle, the woods as so many small trees in a circle, oddly two-dimensional against the flat map of the rest. I passed it to him, ashamed of the wavering lines, the image of the small boy in the sailor-suit still in my mind.

'Thank you,' he said, fingering the card, turning it over to glance quickly at the picture before returning it to his pocket. 'Now you should go. Your sister will be worrying about you.'

As I turned to go he said, 'Come again tomorrow.'

September, 1914

It was nearly the end of the afternoon when we saw them. The sun was a deep, melancholy gold and long shadows slanted across the village square. I was playing with the other village children. We played hopscotch and tag and, although the others were mostly older than me, I was faster for I was wild not to be caught. I was full of the words that James had given me and as I ran I felt as if they might all tumble out of me if I were stopped. I had to stay moving, keep my hands free to twist their embryonic sentences.

The other children were talking of the British soldiers who had been apprehended. André Lacroix said that they were in the woods and the Germans caught them in traps like giant rabbits. Gaston, his brother, said that they were hidden in a cupboard in the house of some old people in Cambrai.

'The Germans searched the house,' he said. 'And they found nothing and they were just leaving when one of the British soldiers in the cupboard sneezed and they found them.'

'No, he farted!' said Jean, laughter

blossoming out of him like a flower.

I wanted to tell them about my soldier, hidden in the barn, about his revolver and the way his hands twisted and taught me how to speak. But I held it like a nut in my stomach and cherished it there. And instead I raised two fingers as a revolver in my hand and squinted as I had seen James do, take position and aim, pulling back my arm with the recoil. Gaston fired back and we all scattered, shooting with rapid stuttering sounds and screeches. Then we saw them.

Two men were being marched up the road. Their uniforms were British. Their hands had been bound and they stumbled as they walked, rifle butts jabbed into their spines when they faltered. Their heads were downcast and it was clear that they had been beaten. The eye of one had been badly cut and the wound still oozed blood.

For a moment I thought he was James.

We were silent now, and still, watching. People came out of their houses to look and they too were silent. One of the men was weaker and he stumbled more often. The soldier behind him kept shouting and prodding at him with the rifle, making him stumble more. Suddenly he fell to his knees and the guard kept yelling at him, kicking. He was trying to get up but the guard was shoving him so much that he could not. Then the other prisoner, the taller of the two, the one with the bleeding eye, broke free and flew at the guard who was now kicking his companion hard. There was a scuffle and for a moment I saw the tall man's eyes as he gripped his adversary and there were tears of rage running down his face. And then there was a shot and a burst of blood from his temple and he collapsed.

Another shot was fired into the air, a warning and there was a yelling of orders and the first man was dragged to his feet, he was whimpering. Curt orders were yelled as the body of the dead soldier was flung on to a cart, shapeless as a scarecrow. His blood stained the cobbles as they moved off over them.

Behind the first group of soldiers came a man and a woman, marching, hands tied. I recognized the woman from the market at Cambrai. They were old, older than my father and they looked bewildered, lost, almost, in the square. They were framed by brickwork and cobbles, but they seemed out of place.

A woman with a baby in her arms cried out and rushed forwards. She ran towards them, but the soldiers pushed her back and her cry joined her child's, rising high like balloons above the red brick square.

They passed by quickly, as if nothing had happened, and the blood of the soldier was soon covered in dust from the feet that passed over it, and the square lay in silence, watching, taking it in. The woman with the baby sobbed in her husband's arms.

After that, the orstkommandant issued a proclamation which Leutnant Voller posted outside the *mairie*. It said that all French and British soldiers hiding in occupied France must hand themselves over, that registers were to be drawn up, stating the names of all those resident at every house and that these were to be posted outside each door. All men between eighteen and sixty must report to the orstkommandant in the village every three days and if any villagers were found to be hiding enemy soldiers the mayor of that village would be shot and the village itself would be fined, or burned down.

And I wondered if there were any other families with a secret like ours, any other soldiers crouching in cellars or barns, breathing soft and low beneath the footsteps of the enemy, their presence a rapid heartbeat just audible beneath their hosts' own, beating out fast panic into the late summer air.

May, 1932

He is sitting on the far side of the café, at the table by the door. Although his back is to me, I know who he is straight away. It has been nearly six weeks since his last visit.

In the square the children are playing, a game of hop-scotch set to a tune I remember from when I was a child.

My father is in the cellar, my sister upstairs, changing the linen. Claire is helping me in the café. She is behind the bar now, pouring a glass of beer for the young man by the door. I see her eyes stray occasionally to where he sits and I wonder if she has recognized him from that day at the cemetery.

Four men sit in the back corner, playing cards. They play for matchsticks which lie in piles over the table. They sit hunched over the game, but they cast occasional glances at the young man by the window.

'So.' One of the men looks up from the game briefly. It is Henri Marcel. 'You're back again, then!'

The young man looks up. 'Yes, yes I am.'

'Got business round here?'

'In a way.' The young man hesitates. 'I'm studying in Paris for a few months.'

'In Paris, eh?' Marcel glances at the other men who laugh, low throaty chuckles.

Claire crosses over to where the young man is sitting, the glass of beer held a little unsteadily in two hands.

'Oh.' Andrew shifts to allow her to put the glass down. 'Thank you.' He catches her eye, smiles. 'Thank you.'

Marcel is watching them.

'Miss,' the phrase Andrew uses is formal, antiquated, marking him out as a stranger, 'I wonder if I could speak to your father?' he says.

Franc Dessenne mutters, 'Her father's dead.'

'Oh, I'm sorry. I . . . ' he fumbles in his pocket, brings out a piece of paper, 'I assumed — I want to speak to Monsieur Léon Fermier. He owns this café?'

'He's my grandfather,' says Claire.

'Of course. I am sorry.'

She stands for a moment, uncertain what to do. She runs a finger along her hairline, a nervous gesture she has picked up without ever knowing from whom she has inherited it.

'He's in the cellar,' she says. 'I'll go and get him.'

'Thank you.'

She moves off and he watches her go, a shadow crossing his face momentarily before he turns back to the drink she has left for him.

'Touching sight, eh?' Henri Marcel addresses this to me.

I turn away and he chuckles, slapping a full hand of cards down on the table.

My father emerges from the cellar. His apron is dusty and he wipes his hands on it before offering one to Andrew.

'Good morning,' he says, his eyes swiftly appraising the stranger.

Andrew stands, takes the proffered hand.

'Monsieur Fermier. Pleased to meet you.' Again the phrase is oddly formal and my father raises an eyebrow before withdrawing his hand. He glances over to the table where the card-game has resumed, then back at Andrew.

'What can I do for you?'

'My name is Andrew Winter. My father was Captain James Winter, King's Own Lancaster Regiment. I'm told that you knew him.'

My father grunts, moves in the direction of the bar, lifts the partition and crosses behind the counter.

'That's no secret around here.'

Andrew has followed him and the two men now stand on either side of the bar. My father takes off the soiled apron, hangs it on a peg, from where he takes a clean one and pulls it over his head. 'What do you want to know?'

'Anything you can tell me.'

My father deftly ties the apron behind his back. His manner is curt, dismissive.

'They told you what happened?'

'We were told very little at the time. Just a telegram to say he was missing. I've been making enquiries, but most of the files about that sort of thing are still closed. Security reasons, they told me.'

My father is half-watching him as he changes one of the optics.

'Well, what do you want to know?'

'When did he come here?'

'August, 'fourteen. Knocked on the door one night. He was injured. We patched him up.'

'Do you remember the exact date?'

'No.' I know that he is lying, for it was the day that the town was captured, but his expression does not change.

Andrew pauses, looks around him. 'Did he stay here?'

My father laughs, so do the men in the corner. Andrew glances back at them.

'Place was swarming with Germans. Nowhere for a man to hide. We put him in the barn.'

'The barn?'

'It's gone now. Outhouse in top field. Nothing left but a few bricks now.'

Andrew nods. 'He was there the whole time?'

My father grunts assent.

'We received a couple of messages,' Andrew says. 'Saying he was safe. Late in nineteen fourteen and early 'fifteen. We don't know how they reached us.'

My father shakes his head. I see him catch Marcel's eye.

'I don't know anything about that.'

Andrew looks down for a moment, then:

'And who knew he was there?'

My father pauses in what he is doing.

'As far as I know, just my family, the doctor. Who knows? Maybe there were others.' He stops. 'This is a small village. People talk.'

'And how did the Germans discover where he was hiding?'

My father says nothing. Shrugs.

'Do you have any idea?'

Silence. My father looks away.

'Did someone tell them?'

'They found him that's all.'

'But do you think someone told them?' His face is red now, eyes bright. 'Is that what happened?'

'Lots of things happened at that time which are best forgotten,' my father says.

Andrew swings around to the men who sit in the corner. 'Did you know my father?' he asks. They look away, say nothing.

He turns again, sees me at the other end of the bar. 'Did you know him?' he says, face red, voice raised.

I am paralysed by his gaze.

'She can't speak.' It is Claire who says it. She is standing behind him.

'Oh.' He turns round quickly, deflated, the colour slowly draining from his cheeks.

'She remembers him though.'

'But you don't?' he asks.

'No, I'm too young to have known him.'

'Of course.' He runs a hand across his brow, which shines now with perspiration. 'I'm — I'm sorry for disturbing your family like this,' he says to my father. 'I didn't mean to. I am very grateful for what you did.'

My father nods.

Andrew glances in the direction of Henri Marcel, inclines his head towards him.

'Good day,' he says.

Marcel grunts a reply.

Andrew turns, takes one more look at Claire before making his way outside.

The bell above the door sounds as he exits. At the table where he sat, the glass of beer remains untouched. My father throws down the cloth which he has been holding and goes out into the back room. Claire looks quickly after him before turning back to watch the figure of the young man disappearing across the square.

'No use making your eyes after that one,' says Franc Dessenne.

Claire turns to him quickly, her face colouring.

'What do you mean?'

'Best ask your mother about that,' he replies, grinning.

Claire glances at me, her face confused.

'Don't mind him.' It is Henri Marcel. 'He thinks he knows more than he does. Happen he's not right about everything.' His gaze meets that of the grinning Franc, who mutters something and returns his eyes to the game. Marcel smiles and glances in my direction. 'Isn't that right, Amélie?'

I look up quickly to catch his gaze, but I do not move my head in reply.

'There's no reason you shouldn't look at that young man, any more than you shouldn't look at me,' he says, addressing Claire now. 'Or Franc here for that matter.' He laughs at this and releases Claire from his gaze, taking a swig of his drink before returning his attention to the game.

Claire is left, standing there, mute as I am and when she takes a step towards me, I turn away.

★   ★   ★

Claire has a stillness about her that my sister never had: the stillness perhaps of a child for whom no father's name appears on the church register. She is not the only child in our village with her mother's name — the Germans left their share of children here too — but Claire has grown up in a house of women and old men, a house where my silence has filtered into every corner, spreading its petals so that the mute alphabet of fingers and skin sounds louder than any other.

I go into the kitchen after Andrew has gone and it is here that Claire finds me. I do not hear her come in and so I am startled when she speaks.

'Who was my father?'

My back is to her and I do not turn around straight away.

She crosses the room until she is by my side. 'You know who he was, don't you?'

I half-turn to her. In this light, she looks older than her sixteen years, blonder even than her mother, with grey-brown eyes. Her hair is tied back with a blue ribbon, the colour of cornflowers. I take her hand in mine, run my fingers over the smooth skin, but form no words there.

'Why doesn't my mother tell me?'

'I don't know,' my fingers say, hesitantly, dealing only in half-truths.

She looks at me, waiting for me to say more. In the light from the window, her face is pale, her eyelashes almost translucent. But my fingers are still now.

After a pause: 'My mother wasn't married to him, was she?'

I shake my head and she mirrors the gesture, silent. Her hand remains in mine, warm, unmoving.

'She told me that he would have married her,' she says after a moment. 'Only he was killed.' She pauses. 'Is that true?'

She glances at her hand, waiting for me to reply. When I do not do so, she lifts her eyes to meet mine.

'You must ask your mother,' my fingers say.

There is silence for a long time and I can feel her turning away from me.

'Is what the young man says true?' she asks, her tone changed, trying to be lighter now, although she has not loosened my hand. 'Did someone betray his father?'

I say nothing.

'Did someone tell the Germans where his father was hiding?'

I allow her hand to drop, move to the table, busy my fingers with crockery. She does not follow me, does not ask the question again. I do not turn around and after a few moments, I hear her leave the room and go upstairs.

October, 1914

There was a couple of soldiers at the end of the lane, lounging against the gate. They seemed drunk from the way their bodies bent. My sister had to pass them to get out to the fields.

I saw one of them, the taller, step out to stop her and he was saying something that made the others laugh. My sister offered no answer but looked away, trying to step to one side in order to pass. But the tall soldier shifted his body to block her way again. There were raised voices and he grabbed at her, playfully, goaded by the laughter of the others, snatching at her basket.

In the basket she had food and dressings for James. The tall soldier tried to take it and her refusal to let it go made him all the more determined. The others joined in, clamouring together, little boys' voices drowning out her protestations.

Suddenly there was a shout from behind and all the soldiers stopped their goading and stood quickly to attention, leaving my sister in possession of the basket, her hair in disarray, pink spots of anger high in her cheeks.

I turned to see Leutnant Voller, bright in the diminishing light, his jacket off, his shirt untucked, not much older than the soldiers who now stood to attention behind my sister.

Voller barked and ordered them away. They turned, moved off, the looseness gone from their bodies now. The late afternoon sun made their shadows long, longer than they were, as if they were more shadow than substance, these soldiers who must soon go and join the fighting. My sister did not move as they filed past her. She stood in the lane, basket in hand, and six feet away stood Voller, the length of his shadow connecting them.

He offered her a curt salute and turned away.

*   *   *

There were posters all around the town now, declaring that French citizens found to be harbouring enemy soldiers would be treated as spies and punished. All cars, bicycles and hunting guns were to be handed over. Pigeons too. In Cambrai, they said, a man was shot by firing squad for disobeying. My father handed over the doves he kept in the top barn lest they be taken for pigeons and bring the outhouse to the Germans' attention.

In the square the games we now played were hiding games, with one of us acting as the German officers and the others the hidden soldiers. I was a British soldier, imagining I was James, and as I stood, breathing behind the crates in the alleyway by the boulangerie, I fancied that this must be how he felt as he listened for noises, the sound of someone approaching the barn: friend or foe.

André Lacroix was searching and I heard his bear footsteps stamping down the alley, the sharp intake of his breaths. He stopped and I could imagine him looking. My own breaths sounded magnified, as if I were under water, they billowed round my ears. He came to the end of the alley, but I was hidden behind the barrels and he did not see me.

I could see him, standing in the middle of the alley, breaths short and quick, eyes bright in the pursuit, looking around. It was dim down there, but a thin shaft of sunshine fell across the cobbles, and, as he stood, half in, half out of the light it made his eyelashes glow white, like Voller's. He imitated Voller's accent as he called out:

'I'm going to find you!' the syllables over-pronounced, vowels distorted. The sound echoed off the walls. He shouted again, looking around. He knew I was near but I remained still, motionless, silent.

⋆   ⋆   ⋆

My father was talking to Henri Marcel in the café. There were German soldiers in the bar, littering the tables, laughing loudly so that they might not hear the sound of gunfire. At the back of the room, Voller sat, poring over a map, smoking, talking to one of the other officers and the orstkommandant, a short, squat man called Roemer.

Marcel stood at the bar, nursing a glass of beer, hunched over it so that the remarks he addressed to my father seemed like idle conversation. My father polished glasses, staring out of the window or looking round the bar, never at Marcel.

I stood in the door to the alcove in the gloom, watching the grey figures lounging in the sunlit bar. It had rained earlier and now the sun retaliated with a brilliant glare that blanched the window panes and made the figures in the square appear to move through a white haze. They were young boys in the bar that day, reservists, and even though they were dressed in grey I could see that most were no older than my sister.

One caught sight of me staring from the

other side of the room. He saw me through the crowd of reservists, raised his arm and held his hands in the shape of a gun, squinting as he pretended to take aim and fire. There was a soft spluttering noise from his mouth and his arm jerked back, imitating the motion of a machine-gun. All was done in deadly earnest, then he lowered his arm and grinned wide, took a slug of his drink and turned back to his companions.

Marcel was staring into his glass, 'Nothing is moving now. It'll be a week at least before things settle down.'

'Come on, Henri, You see how it is.' My father's back was to me and only the low burr of his voice was audible beneath the din, but the urgency was discernible in it.

'I'm saying the same to you as I am to those who want tobacco. Nothing is moving now. Belgium is worse than here and nothing is getting through to Holland.'

Two soldiers stepped up to the bar and ordered drinks. My father went to serve them. One was the soldier who had mimed the machine-gun, but he did not look at me now. He slapped an arm on Marcel's back and greeted him like a friend. He mimed drinking and Marcel shrugged in response, so the soldier indicated that my father should get him one too.

Marcel caught sight of me standing there, leaning against the doorframe, half-hidden in the folds of the fake velvet curtain which separated bar from house. He caught my eye and winked.

My father served the men and pushed a drink towards Marcel then went back to the window.

'You've seen the posters. You know what they say. If they find him, it'll be our necks on the line.'

'Look, if I take your bloody Englishman across the border and I'm caught with him, it'll be me who'll be for it, not you. So we wait.' Marcel's voice was raised and he was looking directly at my father.

There was hostility in the air, rank as dead flesh. My father turned to him.

'So, we wait,' my father said. 'Next week?'

Marcel lowered his eyes to his drink again and said nothing.

October, 1914

He taught me new words every day. The shapes were elegant, smooth. Arcs and curves on my palm which traced patterns on my thoughts. At home, I let my fingers drift over the table-top, over the wooden backs of the chairs, feeling the shapes they made on the smooth surface. In bed, at night, when my sister was asleep, I ran my hand over the sheet between us, watching the indentation it made on the crumpled white linen, sending silent words aloft into the blue night.

His leg had nearly healed now. He showed me the scar, red still and tender, a long indentation in his flesh, a permanent shape etched there, like one of his phrases, running in a red line through his skin.

The weather turned as the month crept towards its close. Brown autumn had set in and the fields were barren, muddy furrows. Only the bare stubble of the razed crops made small patches of colour against the mud. The air was white and the chalky earth glowed blandly with it, so that the trees stood out black in the monochrome landscape.

He was lying down when I arrived. He

stared at the roof, as I had often seen him do, one hand half-covering his forehead, staring blank-eyed at the rafters, listening to the sound of gunfire in the distance. It troubled him, I could see that. His face was covered in shadows, as if the battle was playing out across his thoughts, trapped behind his brows.

He sat up when he saw me, smiled; his face was warm again.

'Hello there,' he rubbed his hand on his trouser leg, held it out to me.

I put down the basket I was carrying and crouched at his side, self-conscious, excited. He rubbed a hand through his hair, waiting. I reached out and took his hand. It was cold today and his skin was red. Slowly, I traced the shape he had shown me for 'Hello'. I looked up. He was watching me and I smiled. My finger moved again. 'How are you?'

'I'm fine,' he said, and it was spoken. He had not removed his hand from mine and I could feel his cold palm as I watched the lips move. 'What about you?'

I just nodded. Then I pointed to the food I had brought and let go of his hand, moved back for a little while. He took it out and ate.

'Do you think you could do something for me?' he asked.

I nodded.

'I need some wire.'

I looked at him, puzzled.

'The soldiers will have some. Or your father, if they haven't requisitioned it all. I only need a bit. About so long.' He held out his arms to show me. 'Can you try to find some for me?'

I shrugged, uncertain.

He grinned and brought my hand up to his mouth in an old-fashioned gesture. I felt his lips press on my skin, warm, his eyes still on mine, smiling.

'Thank you,' he said. And I felt the blood rush to my cheeks, hot, red.

He did not ask any more, but resumed eating. I watched him, wrapped in my own silence. My hand was still warm from the impress of his lips.

There were many things I wanted to ask him. He sat back against the wall, one knee raised, his arm resting on it, head leaning back. Half his face was caught in the light, the other half was in shadow, the stubble on his cheeks coarse and dark. I wanted to trace my finger over the area of bare, exposed skin, feel it smooth and cold beneath my fingers.

He was lost in thought and when I reached to take his hand again, my touch startled him, making him jump. I jumped too, and then he laughed, sudden, unexpected. I had his hand in mine and it was warmer now, as if the food had revitalized him.

Usually I waited for his lead, responded to his questions with the shapes that he had given me to voice my thoughts. This was the first time that I had initiated a conversation. I was slow as I traced the pattern, uncertain. The shape my fingers made was wobbly, unclear. He watched me intently. I did not look up but moved my fingers again, clearer the second time, one shape and then another.

'Age,' then, 'You?' slowly traced with uncertain fingers. I waited a moment then looked up to see if he had understood.

'You want to know how old I am?'

I nodded.

'What do you think?' He had shifted a little so that most of his face was now in the light, and he looked younger, the crow's feet erased temporarily by the sun.

He held his hand out still and I took it again and attempted to shape the numbers he had shown me.

'Thirty?' my fingers asked, uncertain.

He laughed, the same startling sound as before.

'Thanks a lot! Not so old, if you don't mind. Not yet.'

I flushed, tried again, my fingers fumbling. 'Twenty?'

'Better!' He smiled. 'But too young, I'm afraid.'

I struggled to recall the shapes for the numbers in-between, drew the next slowly.

'Twenty-two?'

He shook his head. 'I'm twenty-six,' he said 'Old, huh?'

His eyes were lit, grey lights flecked with brown. I twisted a smile.

'And you?' he asked.

I struggled with the shape, but he made it out.

'Twelve?'

I nod.

He studies me close. 'You don't look so old,' he says, then: 'Go on.' He indicated his hand, leaning forward. 'Ask me some more.'

I took it again, aware of the silence in the barn. The shelling had stopped, a temporary lull in the bombardment. The rooks in the copse were still.

My fingers formed another question, silent words in the hush.

'Family?' they said, 'You?' the question mark in my eyes.

'You want to know about my family?'

I nodded.

This time he took my hand to answer. I watched his long finger move across my palm, felt my hand supported by his, skin on skin.

He traced a single shape. It was the shape

for a boy, and maybe also for brother, I thought. He traced another word. 'One.'

I looked up, nodded, comprehending.

Then his finger moved again. This time: 'Woman' and 'One.'

Confused I took his hand in mine and traced the symbol he had shown me for 'sister'. I raised my eyes in a question.

He shook his head.

I thought of the two shapes: the one for woman, and the one for sister. Perhaps the one he used just now, the one for woman, might also mean a sister. This is what I thought although I was still confused.

Again I asked him: 'Sister?'

And again he shook his head, said nothing for a moment, then used his voice to go on: 'And I had a brother who was killed in an accident. Five years ago now.'

I nodded, noticing that he spoke now with clipped vowels as if it caused him some distress. I was still confused, but I did not question him further.

There was silence for a moment, a slow ticking of time, and then I tried again. This word was hard. I waited a moment, formed the single shape slowly, carefully, my fingers unsteady.

'Mother?' A pause and then: 'Father. You?'

He shook his head, spoke again.

'My father's still alive. My mother died a few years ago.' He seemed intent on my hand, then looked at my face and I felt his eyes searching for something. He paused before saying: 'Like you, I think?' His voice was raised slightly at the end, forming a question, but he said it softly, with the gentle vowels people used when they talked about my mother.

I did not nod, just looked at him. A burst of gunfire sounded in the distance and the crows rose in chill cacophony from the treetops into the frozen sky.

'She died when you were young?' he asked.

He was looking at me and his eyes were grey-brown the colour of dawn in the fields.

'Was that when you stopped talking?'

A word formed somewhere, a bubble rising from a still lake, then sank again. But my hand remained still and I could only nod.

October, 1914

It was nearly the end of October when the rain came. The change came suddenly, unexpected. One day we woke up and the sky was a vivid turquoise, dangerously bright. The air smelt of moisture and there was silent panic in the fields as we worked to bring the last of the harvest in.

But the rain held off all day and by sunset the sky was a brilliant spectrum, opalescent with the imminent deluge.

I went to see James. It was after six when I went, not yet dark, but turning. The curfew was at 7 o'clock, after which time we had to be in our homes. I had the wire he had asked for, wire my father had hidden from the Germans. My father did not know I had it and it was bulky beneath my heavy woollen shawl as I made my way through the darkening fields and along the stream towards the trees. James had not told me what he wanted it for and I had not asked.

When I reached the barn I stopped. There were voices within.

The copse seemed alive, flurries of sound rippling through the dark trees as if the inhabitants knew as well as we did that the rain was coming. I stopped by the doorway to the barn and I could hear it, distinct: a soft peal of stifled laughter, followed by a quick flurry of words. The laughter was unmistakably female.

I pushed the door open just a crack and slipped in. I was conscious of their presence: the sound of their whispered words in the dark. I could not see them, but I heard again the muffled laughter, both of them this time. It tasted sweet that laughter. I stayed very still and I could hear them, and their breath sounded quick, giddy.

The rain had started to fall outside. I moved closer. It was dark in the barn, brown-blue underwater light and at first I could hardly make out the dim figures in the shadows. They were sitting in the corner, side by side. She was half-hidden from my view, but I could see him, see the patterns of light and shade play across his face.

I watched as he took her hand in his. They were both laughing, breathless. I could see their hands, could see the way they twisted together, tentative at first, like a dance, fingers touching, one by one, then palm to palm, skin on skin. Then closer, lips doing what hands did, coming together like their palms.

The sound of the deluge rose, beating heavily now on the roof. The wind heaved the copse into motion so loud that I could hardly hear them any more, their shapeless words drowned out by the current. But I was conscious that they were there — could see his hand touch hers.

My own hands were numb with the cold, stinging in recognition of the ceremony. Then she moved forward a little and in the dim light her hair looked almost white, like that of an old woman.

Panic rose, hot and fast. I turned to leave, quickly, damp pricking at my skin. I went out into the rain, leaving the door open, swinging on its hinges. I dumped the wire by the doorway and ran from the image of their hands intertwined, her hand in his, lips pressed together. A soft peal of laughter followed me as I ran out into the rain.

The fields were empty, the cornfield an expanse of stubble, scattered with stray stalks. It grew muddy now as puddles filled the furrows. In the potato fields there were still patches of green where some of the crop had not yet been brought in, the autumn rain hastening the spread of rot beneath the sods. But I could only think of the way he took her hand, encased it in his own, laughing at the ritual.

I ran back to the house. The back door was open and the rain had already made a horseshoe pattern on the rug inside. The gas-lamps had not yet been lit and so it was dark within. A figure was sitting at the table, facing out towards the rain, a silhouette with only the orange tip of a lit cigarette casting a dim light in the gloom.

He was alone. My father was serving in the bar and my sister was not back yet. The house was empty, apart from Leutnant Voller, seated at the table, smoking, watching the rain.

I halted just outside the door, soaked through now, my hair plastered to my face and my skirt clinging to my legs. I stopped when I saw him and froze beneath the door lintel.

I could not see his features for he was in shadow, but his eyes were brilliant, two white drops reflecting the rain.

'Been playing in puddles?' he asked.

I could think of nothing. Only of her with him, her hands intertwined with his, the same fingers that had traced their speaking patterns on my palm now stroking hers.

For a moment, I was tempted by an impulse. A quick beat of it crossed my mind fleetingly and then, just as quickly, retreated: an impulse to tell Voller. Tell him about

James, about the British soldier hiding in the barn.

The thought receded, but it left a watermark, a faint stain, almost invisible, but there nonetheless, as I stood, water dripping off me, sodden, motionless.

Later, my sister returned, soaked through and shivering with the cold. Her thin limbs were blue and her hair was loose down her shoulders, dripping down her back, white-blonde in the rain. She wrapped herself in a blanket and sat by the fire.

Voller tried to talk to her, but she did not heed him that night. Her thoughts were elsewhere, and he seemed abashed by her presence. Her clothes clung to her and she seemed stripped almost naked by the rain.

I watched her, saw the way she rubbed her hands together to warm them. Palm to palm, running over and over each other, fingers tangled, intertwined. She was beautiful that night, raw, exposed, and I thought, not for the first time, that she looked like my mother.

October, 1914

I watched my sister the next morning: the way she moved about the kitchen, preparing breakfast; the way her knife tugged through the hard grey bread; the way she poured tea into the mugs, hot and strong, for there was no sugar now, only a little boiled beetroot to sweeten the bitter black brew. She put the bowls down carelessly, not looking at me.

She was distracted, her movements more jerky than usual, the beauty of the previous evening all gone now, replaced by a gracelessness as she lifted the hem of her apron to rub her shining brow.

I did not eat my bread and I barely sipped the tea she gave me. I was aware, after a few moments that she was watching me. I looked up, caught her gaze.

'Are you sick?' she asked, her glance penetrating.

I shook my head.

She came over. Her hand went to my brow with a brisk motion. I looked down, but she kept it there for a moment and I could feel its hot impress on my skin.

'You've not got a fever,' she said.

Her fingers ran along the line of my hair for a brief moment. The gesture was intimate and I looked up quickly, but she moved away.

'Don't play with your food. There's little enough of it,' she was saying, busying herself once again with the fire, her thoughts departed from me now, elsewhere.

So, I sat, staring at the grey bread in front of me, aware of the sting of her touch on my brow.

★ ★ ★

James was reading when I got to the barn. A book I hadn't seen before. French, with a battered brown cover. I wondered how he had got hold of it.

He looked up when I came in. Smiled.

'You're early.'

I did not go towards him, but hung back, nervous around him today.

'Thanks for the wire,' he said.

I nodded. Still unmoving.

'Why didn't you come in and say hello when you brought it?'

I shrugged.

He put the book down, looked at me, puzzled.

'Do you want to sit?' he said.

I shrugged again, but moved a little closer,

not to my usual spot, but a few yards further away.

'Is something wrong?' he asked.

I looked away, aware of his eyes on me.

'I see.' He spoke slowly, ran his hand over the leather cover of the book that lay beside him. Then his voice changed. 'They say there's no getting out across the lines at the moment. There's no break from here to the coast,' he said.

He leant against the wall, took out the silver cigarette-case which I had come to recognize and extracted a cigarette.

'Your father says there's a man who can get me out through Holland.'

He took out a box of matches and attempted to light one. It was damp and it failed to catch on the first few attempts. He struck again and this time it fizzled into an acrid flame. He lifted it to the cigarette which hung from his lips.

'I reckon it's my only chance.'

I watched him for a moment, watched the way he inhaled the smoke, held it in his lungs then exhaled, his thoughts elsewhere, grey eyes thoughtful, distant. He shook out the match to extinguish it.

I wanted to go to him, to touch his hand, ask him what he meant, if he was planning to leave, but I remained motionless.

'I'm putting your family in danger,' he said. He looked at me and I held his gaze. 'I have to go. I'm sorry.'

I stood up quickly, clumsily in my haste to get away. I heard him call out after me as I left the barn, but I did not look back.

June, 1932

The next time Andrew comes the café is full. There are day-trippers, come with one of those excursions to the battlefields that have become so popular in the last few years. They pass through the village in autobuses, on the scenic route from Ypres to the Somme. Most do not stop here, but carry on to Arras, Beaumont Hamel, Vimy Ridge, but on hot days sometimes there is one that pauses in the village square and the passengers pile into the café for refreshments. Mostly it is English that they speak, but even I can hear that there are different lilts to their voices. I have heard that families come from as far afield as Canada and Australia to see where their loved ones are buried.

They sit in small groups, dotted around the tables, talking quietly, not looking around, dressed in black. There are families and couples mostly: men supporting their wives; children too young to have known their lost fathers; cousins; uncles wearing black armbands; the odd veteran with a sewn-up sleeve or trouser-leg. But *they* always come alone. The veterans always come alone.

Today's group is much the same as the others which have been here. There are maybe a dozen of them in all. Although we have put out tables on the pavement, they sit inside, coats and jackets firmly kept on. He stands out because he is young — not a veteran but alone, sitting at the same table by the door where he sat last time. Amidst the low talk and cigarette smoke, I notice him straight away.

My sister is taking orders from the tables, assisted by the tour guide who is translating for her, and so she does not see him.

The sun is milk-warm, struggling into one of the first days of the summer. The door is open and the light pours through the big front windows on to the wooden floor, the lettering on the dusty panes casting a sloping shadow on the boards in giant copperplate. It has been raining for the last few days and the windows are grimy, so the light is dusty as it falls on my sister.

I wonder as I watch her move about the room in old clothes — a shapeless cardigan wrapped around her — whether these people look at her and think she is beautiful. Perhaps now she is one of those people of whom one thinks: *She must have been a beauty, once.* She looks ordinary in her old skirt and flat shoes, her thin hair pulled back tight so that her face looks angular, and her curves are hidden by the cardigan. But at least two of the men look at her as she serves them, with a kind of surprise, as if they hadn't expected to find beauty in a place like this, and they allow their eyes to follow her for a moment as she moves off.

She comes to his table last. He glances up quickly, not taking her in, not recognizing her.

'Nothing to eat, thanks,' he says. 'Just a coffee. No milk.'

If she is surprised that he has spoken in French she does not show it. She writes down his order and starts to move off.

'Oh.' He looks up quickly, calls after her. She turns back to him. He is looking up now and his face is open, caught in the light from the window so that the shapes of the lettering fall on his features. 'I wonder, could you help me. I am looking for a place near here.' He pulls out a crumpled envelope with a crude map drawn in pencil on the back. He straightens it out, passes it to my sister. She takes it from him.

He has noticed now that she is beautiful and he is addressing her with the courtesy men extend to attractive women.

'It's a place that has family significance. I thought while I was passing through I would go and take a look.' He has not recognized her.

'It is just up the path behind the church,' she says, 'behind the copse. It's derelict now.'

'How long will it take me to get there?'

'Five minutes at most.'

'And this place?' He points to another place he has marked in pencil.

My sister bends close to see it and their faces are almost side by side.

'The quarry?' she says. 'That is further away. Twenty minutes walk at least.' She turns to go.

'You're Thérèse, aren't you.'

My sister only half-turns back to him. The sun has disappeared behind a cloud and she stands in shadow as she answers:

'I have to see to these orders.'

She goes quickly to the bar and through the archway. He stands up to follow her and crosses to the counter. He can see her, in the alcove, cutting bread.

'You knew my father,' he says, having to speak louder, so that a few of the day-trippers look up, startled from their own private reveries for a moment.

She half-looks round at him.

'Did I?' she says.

'Captain James Winter. He was here during the war. Your family sheltered him.'

'Yes,' she says. 'Yes, I remember him.'

She has crossed to the other side of the alcove now. He can no longer see her.

'What was he like?' Andrew asks.

I think this must halt her for a moment for the sound of motion stops.

'You knew him. What was he like?' Andrew says again.

'He was no different from any other soldier.'

Andrew has moved along the bar so that he is right by the entrance to the alcove now.

'I never knew him. I would like to have known what kind of man he was.'

A pause.

'He was a good man.' She is still unmoving.

'Was he?'

'Yes, he was.'

A low murmur of talk underscores this exchange, from the groups in black scattered about the tables.

'And did he ever talk of me?' Andrew asks.

'Yes, he did.' She emerges from the alcove holding a plate of food. 'He had a photo of you,' she said, facing him now, plate in hand. 'He said it was taken just before he left. He always kept it with him.'

Andrew is watching her. He says nothing, but I can see a vein in his temple throbbing.

'The night he disappeared,' she continues,

'he didn't take it with him. It was found afterwards, in the barn.'

She puts down the plate and reaches under the counter, pulls out an old biscuit tin in which my father keeps papers and letters. She opens it, fingers through its contents and takes out a small square of photographic card. She places it on the bar in front of Andrew. I recognize the photo, yellowing now, but still clear: a little boy in a sailor-suit.

'He wouldn't have gone without it,' she says. 'That's how we knew.'

Andrew looks at her, quickly, his face red with emotion.

'Knew what?'

'That the Germans had found him.'

Andrew is fingering the photograph. I can see him only in silhouette, but his cheeks are red and his jaw set.

'Thank you,' he says, only half-meeting my sister's eye. He puts the picture in his pocket, the movement clumsy. 'Thank you very much.' He extends his hand. She lifts hers to meet his. The gesture is formal, out of place. I watch as their hands meet and recall for a second the old jealousy.

He picks up his coat and hat and goes out into the street. My sister watches him and so do I.

It is a moment before she becomes aware

of me standing behind her. She half turns towards me as she speaks.

'I knew,' she said. 'I knew that he was married. Not right from the start, but I did know.'

She is still holding the tin of letters, but she closes it now, puts it away.

'I knew he had a son too.'

She stands for a moment, unmoving, and then she picks up the plates of food and takes them over to the couple in the corner.

November, 1914

There were new notices now, pinned up outside the *mairie*. It was forbidden to display visible lights in houses at night, to hang out laundry, to light fires in the fields or to travel to the next village without a pass. Adults were not permitted to gather in groups of more than three, and we were not even to look at the aircraft which flew over regularly now. Orstkommandant Roemer was convinced that messages were being passed to free France and every measure was taken to stem the flow of information.

That evening the fields were a sea of orange, a screaming sunset staining the mist which still hung in the hedgerows. From my window the view was layered, orange light, white mist and then the smudged charcoal on the margins of the fields.

I had not seen James that day. I had been in the fields with the other children and a handful of women, grubbing out the last of the beet with frozen fingers, hunched backs bent over the sods. My hands were red-raw and numb from scrabbling in the frosted earth and my back ached with a sharp throbbing pain. I was damp through to my bones. The fog had infiltrated my clothing, seeping into the fabric and freezing there so that it clung to my skin and stung with cold. My hair was plastered to my pinched cheeks as I pushed open the back door to the house.

I stopped on the threshold, door open behind me, the brilliant sunset throwing its gilt colours across the stone floor. Seated by the fire was Henri Marcel. There was no one else in the room.

I turned slowly to push the door to, my eyes still on him. My dress clung so close to my legs that I felt indecent, exposed. He had a hip-flask in his hand and he had kicked off his boots to warm his feet in front of the fire.

'Evening,' he said, his voice thick, though whether it was with liquor I could not tell.

I said nothing. Stood there, looking at him.

'Well, you might as well come in.'

I could not stay by the door for ever, dripping. I put down my basket and stepped towards the fire.

'Aren't you the quiet one!' he said. I was only a few feet away from him, aware of his eyes on me.

I nodded. Standing before the fire, shivering, unmoving.

'I'm waiting for your father,' he said eventually.

He scratched his stomach and I watched out of the corner of my eye as he took a small packet of tobacco out of his coat pocket and proceeded to stuff some into his pipe.

'So', he said, prodding the brown twists into the bowl. 'How's your soldier today?'

I looked up, startled.

'Oh, you'll look at me now, will you. Pretty face you've got on you, eh.' He held my gaze, then returned to his pipe. 'I hear he's been turning a few heads.' The words seemed to toy with me and I felt my brow pucker, felt confused, self-conscious.

'You don't want to go screwing up your face like that, case the wind changes and you're stuck that way,' he said and I could smell the alcohol on him now, like the smell of my father's clothes after he had been serving in the café. 'You don't want your soldier catching you with that face on you or he'll be finding himself a new sweetheart.'

The catch lifted on the door and made me jump. But it was only the wind which made the door bang to now, loose on its hinges. Marcel got up, pipe in hand, not yet lit, and pushed the door closed, clicking the latch firmly into place.

'He's going, you know,' he said, sitting down, reaching in his coat pocket for a match which he struck against the hearth, bringing it close to his face, cradling it over the bowl of his pipe with one rough brown hand.

I was watching him closely, waiting for him to continue. He took his time, puffing in short indrawn breaths until the tobacco was lit and then inhaling deep, holding the smoke in his lungs while he fixed his eyes on me.

'Well, you'd better find yourself a new boyfriend quick, 'cos he's off tomorrow. I'm to take him through to Holland your father says. Too much of a liability. I daresay that's not the way you see it, though — eh?' He laughed, inhaled again.

I felt something rise to my gullet and then my throat contracted and I stared hard at the fire spluttering in the grate. My hands were sore and itchy, chilblains starting to form on the swollen ends of my fingers.

The door from the bar swung open at that moment and a rush of voices flooded in. Boyish laughter and a few bars of a song, sung high and clear, cutting through the mist. It was a chorus of home, evident from the long wistful notes of the refrain. I had heard this one before.

Marcel had not moved, but sat there smoking, watching me.

'Perhaps it's for the best though,' he said. And then: 'For your sister's sake and all.'

November, 1914

I was aware of my sister getting out of bed. Even in the darkness, with my back turned to her, I could feel the movement of the mattress, the soft tread on the floorboards. It was dark still and the clock on the mantelpiece said four o'clock. The mist still clung to the house muffling the sound of her movements as if she were under water.

I could see her at the foot of the bed, dressed only in her slip, which glowed white in the dark room. I lay still and watched her. I could see her reflection in the mirror, her bare shoulders caught intermittently in the moonlight, which cast lunar shadows across the room. Her hair was loose, milky strands on her bare skin. She pulled a blouse over her slip and then a skirt over that. She was silent as she moved, her feet light on the boards and her motions swift.

She pulled on her shawl, picked up the wooden clogs she wore in the fields, bundled her hair under a scarf. I remained still the whole time, keeping my breath shallow, not wanting her to know I was awake.

And when she was gone, I lay there,

stranded on the big white bed, staring still at the empty shadows on the mirror, the geometrical shapes of furniture, the white curve of the chair, the grey blotches on the wall opposite and the space where her shape had been.

And I heard the latch lift on the door downstairs and sound of her footsteps on the gravel and I knew where she was going.

★   ★   ★

Nobody told me that he had left, but I knew that he had. My sister was altered by his departure. I saw her pause in the middle of tasks — her hands in a bowl of water, a cloth in her hand, her arms full of linen — she would stop and there was a quick indrawn breath, and she would be still a moment, holding it, controlling the breath before she released it, slowly, her body tensed with the effort, before she resumed what she had been doing.

I watched her and I longed to take her hand and trace a pattern of consolation on the soft skin of her palm, to etch a piece of him into her and so join us with the words he taught me, but she seemed closed into herself, too distant to touch, and the shapes were meaningless without him, simply random patterns divested of meaning, the silent alphabet hushed now that there was no one to hear it.

*   *   *

James had been gone for over a week. It was evening and Voller had just eaten. He was late that evening and so he ate alone. When he had finished, instead of getting up from the table immediately, as he usually did, he remained where he was, watching my sister as she cleared the table. My father was in the café. There were just the three of us.

He watched her for some time and then said:

'You are sad, I think?' His French was better than it had been when he first arrived but the inflexions were still unfamiliar.

She glanced over, shook her head, turned away.

'Perhaps there is something you need. Something you cannot obtain?' He did not look at her as he spoke but at the table where his hand tapped gently against the grain.

'No.' She said this quietly.

If he was surprised at her response, he did not show it, but still he did not show any sign of moving.

My sister crossed the room, picked up a

basket of darning and took her usual place by the fire, self-conscious in Voller's presence. Usually he went out, to the café or to the *mairie*, where the orstkommandant had set up his headquarters. His presence that night was unwanted, unfamiliar.

'When the war is over, things will be better,' he said, still not looking at my sister, his fingers curling and uncurling as he spoke, a nervous gesture, repetitive. I watched the way they stretched, tentatively and recurled again. 'There will be no more shortages.'

'No?' my sister said. There was no real note of challenge in her voice.

'I studied in Paris before the war, you know.' He looked up then, wanting to catch her eye. 'I loved the French authors: Balzac, Maupassant, Molière!' His accent was still guttural, illfitting with the rounded French vowels. He spoke quickly, as if he were embarrassed.

'I don't know them,' said my sister. The fire was low and her face was mainly in shadow. Her needle stabbed the fabric and hovered, there was no rhythm to her sewing that night.

'My mother was born in France. She talked of it often.' Again, he spoke quickly. He had removed his hand from the table and it now lay on his lap. 'She was born in Mons.'

'I heard what your army did to Mons,' said

my sister, sharply. She looked up, briefly, a challenge in her eyes. 'Does your mother know about that?'

'My mother is dead.'

Silence. My sister said nothing. Her needle stabbed at the fabric she held in her hand.

'This is war,' Voller said, his voice quiet. 'We are not barbarians, but in war such things sometimes are necessary, perhaps.'

'Are they?' My sister looked up again, caught his gaze and held it this time.

'I was sick in my heart when I saw what they did to Mons, but the quicker the war is won, the sooner the rebuilding can begin. A quick victory is necessary. For this we must be harsh. When the war is over, there will be the time for kindness.' This was all said to her, but she had looked away.

He stood then, pushing his chair back noisily. He excused himself and left, and as he roughly pushed open the door I saw that his face glowed red against his white-blond hair.

11th November, 1914

The fighting was heavy in Belgium, near Ypres and Gheluvelt, we heard. The German troops who were being moved up north told us this and the village was quieter now that they were gone. But there had been fighting in this part of the front line too over the last few days: a skirmish west of here that had lasted twenty-four hours, during which we were kept awake by the incessant rattle of the guns and whining of the shells. We were told that the British losses had been by far the greatest, but the German boys who returned along the lanes were hollow-eyed, blood-splattered and silent. And there were many who came limping or on stretchers, their arms, legs, eyes bandaged clumsily, red roses blooming through the white; and some whose faces we had come to know did not return at all.

The café was full of soldiers the evening that Magali came in. We had seen them march back from the front earlier that day, covered in mud, marching through solid rain. This evening there was a kind of crazed hilarity to them, as if they had left something of themselves behind there in the fighting, without which they were untuned, unable to settle.

It was nearly seven o'clock, but it had been dark outside for a couple of hours already. The oil-lamps created yellow doubles of themselves in the darkened windows and the soldiers were reflected too, their ghostly *doppelgängers* luminous in the black glass, bathed in gold light but silent, unlike the raucous originals within. I watched the shifting forms in the darkened windowpane and in my mind I thought that these were the ones who had not returned, the golden forms of the lost men, figured in the glass. Silent.

My sister helped to serve that evening, because it was so busy. I was not supposed to go into the café at night, but I hid in the doorway as I often did, just inside the alcove, where the food was prepared and from where I could see but remain unseen. The soldiers were drunk, but they were not rowdy that night. They wanted to laugh and to sing, but the notes sounded forced, uneasy.

There was one soldier I noticed in particular, a boy with glasses and a graze on his left cheek where something sharp had caught him just below the eye. A lucky escape. When he lifted the drink in his hands, the shaking was so bad that he could barely keep himself from spilling the liquid, hardly get it to his mouth.

'Don't mind him,' one of the other soldiers said to my sister, slapping the boy with the glasses on the back. 'He killed his first man today, is all.' Then he turned away, to join in a joke one of the others was making, and my sister turned away too, unable to watch those trembling hands spilling the drink over the bar.

The sound of German voices filled the night. My sister was part of it too: she moved in and out of the tables, clearing glasses, her body weaving amongst the figures of the men, but touching none of them. Their eyes followed her as men's eyes always did, and their comments twisted threads about her through which she moved unheeding, brushing them aside like cobwebs.

The large clock that hung on the back wall seemed to move slowly that night. The large ornate hands stroked the thick black numerals, figuring the hour of seven and slipping between quarter to and the hour, scarcely appearing to move.

I did not see the café door open, nor Magali coming in. She must have stood there for a moment before the men by the entrance became aware of her presence. Women rarely came into the café at night and it was nearly time for the curfew. Most villagers were inside their homes already. There were a few catcalls, but she ignored them and crossed the room, coming over to the bar where my sister stood. Her motions were hurried, self-conscious.

She was wrapped up well, with a shawl pulled tight over her head and shoulders. Her face, even then, in that light, was fretted with shadows and she looked thinner now than she had before the Germans came.

The soldiers moved apart to let her pass to the bar. She moved quickly, not looking to either side of her, and I could see the gas-lamps reflected in her eyes. Amber, the colour of fear.

Hurriedly, Magali removed a bottle from her coat pocket. A piece of paper was wrapped around it. She gave it to my sister.

'For Amélie,' she said, audibly, so that the soldiers around could hear her. 'For her cough.' And then something else, whispered now, quickly, barely audible beneath the noise of the bar.

The soldiers around us had started up an old folk-tune, sung rowdily, in mocking voices. Although I did not understand the words, I knew that their eyes wrapped lewdly round the two women as they sang and I could catch only a few words of what Magali was saying.

'He's back. He came back this afternoon,' I heard.

Laughter as the song rolled into a chorus.

Then: 'Take this to him.' And then she turned to go, quickly, her movements nervous.

There was a loud burst of laughter from the other side of the room, and a catcall as one of the soldiers clambered up on the table, shouting out the chorus. The others were crowding around, calling, cheering.

Magali was half-way to the door by now but my sister stopped her, grabbing her arm.

'Where is he?' she asked, her eyes gold, like cat's eyes.

'Same place, said Magali. 'There was nowhere else.' Then: 'I have to go.' She turned quickly and pulled open the door. The bell tingled and I had a brief view of the dark tunnel of the night before the door swung to and the chorus of the song started up.

The room was hot and the young men's voices rose high as if they sang to block out the remembered clamour of the guns and the wails of their dying companions still ringing loud in their ears.

★ ★ ★

My heart was racing by the time I reached the barn. The moon was full and the sky was cloudless.

It was past the curfew, and as I approached the barn I could hear voices from within. I stopped by the half-open doorway. There was a light also; a candle flickering in the darkness, by which I could make out two dimly shifting figures.

A voice I did not recognize at first was whispering in urgent tones. 'They have most of their army engaged up in Flanders. There won't be a better time than now.'

Then I heard James's voice, quiet, but insistent. 'It can't be helped. I have to stay.'

The second voice cut in quickly, the low guttural now recognizable as that of Henri Marcel.

'Well, it's your look-out then.'

'Yes, it is.'

There was movement within, a further exchange which I did not catch, for they were moving towards the doorway and I darted out of the way so as not to be seen. I pressed myself against the barn wall, feeling damp seep through my clothes to my skin as I watched Marcel's squat figure emerge and move off into the night.

The candle was still lit within the barn and when I moved back to the doorway I could see its dim glow in the corner. I pushed the door open and moved slowly in the direction of the light. James was sitting in the pool of yellow cast by the candle, dressed in his uniform, just as he had been the first time I saw him. Now he was looking over some papers. His breath clouded the air in front of him and, in the gloom, only the contours of his face were visible.

I shifted slightly and he looked up quickly, startled, shoved the papers hastily out of sight and swung the candle in my direction.

I froze, caught in its guttering light. Then he laughed,

'What are you doing here?' He sounded half-angry, half-amused.

'Come here,' he said, tucking the papers quickly into the inside pocket of his jacket, but not before I had seen that among them were two photos: the one I had seen before, of the small boy in the sailor-suit, my sketch of the quarry on the back of it; and another, with three figures in it, which I could not make out in the darkness.

'You shouldn't be here. If they catch you out this late, there'll be trouble.'

I moved closer and squatted down next to him, cold without my shawl, which I had forgotten in my haste. He pulled off his jacket and put it round my shoulders.

'Here,' he said. Then, softer, 'It's good to see you.'

He had taken a cigarette out of his pocket and he was lighting it. They were Dutch cigarettes — I could see that by the packet — the kind that Henri Marcel sold to the soldiers.

'There was no way out' he said. 'There were roadblocks at the borders, sentries everywhere. Nothing for it but to come back.' He inhaled quickly and the lit end of the cigarette glowed orange. 'Besides,' he grinned and blew a white cloud into the shadows, 'I missed you all!'

I smiled, feeling the prickly wool of his jacket against my skin.

'So,' he said, 'I reckon you are going to have to put up with me for a bit longer, after all!'

★   ★   ★

I went back the long way, through the woods and by the stream, so as not to be seen. As I approached the back of the house, I heard voices in the yard. I stopped, a little distance away. My father was with another man and they were talking in low whispers. I could not get back into the house without passing them, and the only other way in was through the café, which was still full of German soldiers, although by now it was well past closing-time.

From the square came a brief burst of noise as the café door swung open and ejected some of the soldiers out into the night. My sister's raised voice was briefly audible as she tried to persuade the remainder to leave. I could hear the departing soldiers turn down the lane where I was standing, and I ducked into the alley at the side of the house, my heart beating loudly in my chest.

I could hear my father's voice, an urgent whisper on the other side of the wall: 'Why the hell did you bring him back, Henri?'

And then a second voice, thick, perhaps with liquor: 'He didn't give me a bloody choice.' He insisted. 'What was I to do?'

'Stop him. You should have stopped him.'

My father was cut off by the sound of the group of drunken soldiers passing along the lane behind the house. They were laughing, but it was the same manic laughter I had heard earlier in the café, and it rang hollow in the dark night.

I pressed myself into the shadows as the soldiers passed close. One of them glanced into the alley where I stood, hardly daring to breathe. I felt sure that he must see the whites of my eyes, sparkling in the dark, but he turned away, stumbling and muttering something under his breath and I saw that he was the soldier from the bar, the one who had been unable to hold his drink. The one who had killed his first man that day.

The two men in the yard were silent as the soldiers passed. The conversation did not resume for a minute or two, during which I could hear their low breathing. When they spoke again it was more quietly than before and I had to strain to hear them.

'Why the hell did he want to come back?' It was my father.

'How should I know?'

'Didn't he say anything?'

'Not to me. I guess he has his reasons.' The tone was offhand.

'What do you mean?'

'There has to be a pretty good reason for a man to risk his life coming back here. Something pretty special. Or *someone*.' The last words formed a question, the whisper sibilant, leaving it unanswered in the cool night air.

There was silence. I heard Henri Marcel cough, and spit loudly on the floor.

My father said something which I didn't quite catch, then his voice rose as he said: 'He'd better get out of here soon, or I'll turn him in myself.'

Marcel cut in with something I couldn't

hear and the conversation continued at this tone, inaudible now, so that my father's words were the last I heard and they hung in the night air like a warning.

★   ★   ★

It was exactly ninety-nine days since the war had begun and, although none of us knew it then, it would be four years to the day before it was over. Later we would learn how, further north, the Kaiser's army mounted the final attack of the battle of Ypres that day and an outnumbered and near-broken British army performed the unthinkable, holding them off in some of the most desperate fighting of the war. It was to be the last serious offensive of the winter, and the last chance for the Germans to deal a decisive blow to the British. One more push and the battle — and the war itself — would have been over. Instead the British held on and the Germans, not knowing how close they had been to victory, retreated to lick their wounds.

Both sides lost heavily that winter, although the reports we heard spoke only of British and French casualties. The winter was setting in and attacks would continue, but not on the same scale. A new kind of warfare had begun, and, as men dug in like animals across the fields of Flanders and northern France, we all began to realize that this war would not be over by Christmas.

June, 1932

As you get closer to where the front line once was, the land becomes more scarred, the even rolling fields give way to a pock-marked, lunar landscape, craters filled with stagnant water, shell-holes, rusting barbed wire. Some areas are still fenced off, and government notices flap from wire, warning of undetonated mines buried like obscene bulbs beneath the sods. Charred tree-stumps like blackened human hands reach out from the mud, telling where a thicket once stood, and mounds of rubble lining the cratered roads are all that remain of the hamlets whose names became synonymous with the front line.

They are still clearing the land, still unearthing remnants: helmets, boots, mess-tins, letters, photographs, bones. Everywhere the clearing goes on and the seagulls reel in bold arcs above the teams of workers who still sometimes turn up body parts the stench of which fills the air round Arras, Bapaume, Beaumont Hamel, the Somme. Only the cemeteries have any order to them, neat plots of green amongst the chaos, their rows extending day on day as the unknown soldiers continue to be harvested from the gouged earth.

A few days after Andrew's visit, I go back to the cemetery where James now lies. The fields in which it stands were behind the lines so the land here was not so ravaged and its unruffled air contrasts starkly with the pitted landscape of the front.

There are cemeteries outside every village, by the roadsides, these little square plots with their rows on rows of white. They are scattered now all over the countryside of northern France, marking out the long line of the Western front which stretched up to Flanders in the north and Switzerland in the south.

Today the weak June sunlight strains through the clouds, bathing the fields in a bland white light. I approach the cemetery from the road and stand for a few moments on the grassy verge looking over at the neat symmetry of its low white walls, at the shadow cast by the solitary yew-tree growing in the corner.

There is somebody there already. A solitary figure standing amongst the graves. A woman, in a dark coat and hat. She remains still, hands folded in front of her, as if in contemplation of one of the tombstones.

I make my way down the rutted path that leads across the fields, my eyes on the solitary figure. She does not move. As I approach the low stone wall, I slow down. I can see her only from behind, but I am sure it is she. She stands in front of his grave, looking down, head slightly bent.

I lift the low iron gate, which creaks on its hinges, and step on to the smooth green rug of the grass. There is order here, amongst the serried rows of graves. I am only a few feet away from her now, but I would not call her name even if I could, for she would not hear me. I step towards her instead, to touch her on the arm, softly, so as not to frighten her, but as I move to do so she turns and we are standing face to face.

It is not she. Perhaps it was foolish to think that she would make the trip from England again so soon after the last, to think that she would come without her son. I feel a trickle of disappointment, like cold water in my stomach, as the woman who is not James's wife points to the grave which lies beside his and says, 'My brother,' in hesitant French, and then moves past me, leaving me standing alone on the damp grass, facing James's grave.

The headstone has been engraved now. The families of the dead can pay for a line of verse, or a piece of scripture. They say there is one near Poelkapelle with a line of music etched on it. Most of the verses are saccharine, sentimental. The stuff of greetings-cards, my sister says. 'They might as well read: 'Wish you were here,' for all the originality of sentiment they show,' she once said. But at least there is an attempt, a reaching out, something other than the bald uniformity of the French crosses. We all have our own ways of speaking to the dead, and chocolate-box sentiments are no better or worse than any other perhaps, if they bring relief.

There is no attempt at poetry on James's grave, just his name, date of birth and regiment, along with the regiment insignia. Then just four words: *We will miss him*, almost obscured by a miniature rose planted at the base.

But these are not what catch my eye. It is what they have inscribed after his name: 'WINTER, Capt. James Edward, MC.' This is what jumps out at me. It seems incongruous, out of place. A mistake, perhaps.

The woman who left has not closed the gate properly, and it swings to and fro on its hinges, banging against the gatepost with a harsh metallic thud. I lay down the flowers I have brought for him and make my way over to the exit. By the stone gatepost there is a casement containing a record book: a register of those buried here. I turn to the entry for James. It gives his name, rank and number, and the name of his regiment, but for date of death it simply reads '1915'. It gives his home address, too, the same one that Andrew left on the scrap of paper in the café, and it refers to his wife, Miriam, and son, Andrew. And there, again, is the reference to the Military Cross. No more than the bare initials after his name, no official citation, no details about the circumstances in which it had been awarded. Simply: WINTER, Capt. James Edward, MC.

My fingers linger on these initials, tracing each letter, as if by touch I might uncover the answers to the questions they raise.

I glance back at the headstone before I leave the cemetery. There is something I haven't noticed, beside the rose bush: a posy of flowers, almost hidden in the grass. They have been there a few days and are wilted now. They are tied with a piece of ribbon, which is fading now, like the petals. A blue ribbon, the colour of cornflowers.

December, 1914

We played out in the square. Hop-scotch and skipping games, with new words to the old tunes, lyrics for the war. No one knew who thought up the new words, but quickly they stuck: *January, February, March, April, May. How many Kaiser's Men did you kill today? One, two, three, four* . . . Jumping higher and higher with each count. The soldiers watched us as they sat smoking in the square. Sometimes they even cheered us on as we jumped higher and higher, tallying up the numbers of their dead. They understood nothing of what we sang and so we jumped over and over: *Fifteen, sixteen, seventeen, eighteen* . . .

There had been frost on the ground for a week and the fields were iron, glistening with the rime. In the trenches to the east, the weather killed as many men as the guns, and frostbite took fingers and toes; freezing mud rendered corpses solid so that the dead could not even be buried, but lay stiff, side by side with their former comrades.

And we played in the square, childish games overlaid with the lyrics of death and dying. All morning we played, and the game became more elaborate: *Shoot him from behind, Bayonet him through, Two at a time.* These instructions accompanied various feats: jumping backwards, with hands on head, with a twist. Over and over the chant rolled, the words echoing in the ice-cold air so that I felt as if they were etched into me. The warm steam from our breaths stained the air white so that the letters seemed to have been traced there in the mist, dancing, clear and visible, in the cold air.

There was no great fanfare when the prisoners came. We heard the sound of troop movement in the lanes all the time and so the slow thud was familiar and the game went on. But when they reached the square, we saw that these were different. They were not dressed in the uniform grey, but in khaki: row upon row of muddy, bloodstained khaki.

They were British prisoners, captured in a raid on the line four miles north of here, some dressed in the same uniform James had been wearing when I first met him. Downcast they marched, exhausted. They were splattered with the blood of their companions and they did not sing as they had done the last time we had seen them, back in August, when they had marched eastwards down these lanes. Those summer days were long forgotten; these were not the men who had sung back then — they had fallen long ago.

People came out of the houses. I heard one woman call out, 'Chin up love!' and one soldier looked up and replied in English, saying something which we did not understand but which made the other men laugh.

Another woman tried to pass a loaf of bread to one of the prisoners, but she was roughly knocked back by a German guard and the loaf fell on the muddy pavement, caught beneath trampling feet and lost.

But the rest of us were silent, for we had been told that we were not to talk to prisoners, or make contact of any kind with them.

We did not run beside them as we had done back in August. Instead, we stood and watched, the game abandoned, the rope trailing on the ground. I watched them march, row on row, tossing the odd comment from one to another occasionally but mostly silent, grim, looking down as they trudged, dragging exhausted bodies along with them.

I felt a hand on my shoulder, something thrust into my pocket, a low voice behind me whispering, 'Take this, quick. Don't look at me.'

Short breaths, the sound of the marching

soldiers, a shout from an angry guard and one man falling as a blow landed on his temple, my own heartbeats echoing.

The German Hussars were dispersing the people who had gathered in the square with shouts and shoves. I was pushed roughly against the person behind me, felt contact with coarse material, warm flesh.

'Give it to James,' a voice was whispering in my ear. 'Next time you see him.' It was a woman's voice. 'Don't show it to anyone or tell anyone about it.'

I turned quickly, but she had already moved away. I could see her retreating figure pushing back through the crowd that had gathered.

I was breathing hard. I put my hand in my pocket and I could feel the piece of paper inside. I was still aware of the warm impress of her fingers on mine, the urgency of her tone.

The soldiers pushed us back now, roughly, with the butts of their rifles, yelling at us to clear off, and I could see her face in my mind, caught for a second before she turned away.

I had recognized her straight away. For it was Magali Legrange.

When I reached the barn, the door was open, swinging on its hinges, although there was no breeze. I stopped, listening out for his breathing, but I could hear nothing.

I went in slowly, conscious that something was wrong. I crossed the barn, aware of the sound of my footsteps on the earth floor, the letter in my pocket. Something clattered beneath my feet and I let out an involuntary cry. The sound echoed up in the rafters. I looked down to see what my foot had caught. A lump of metal, once part of a yoke, had fallen from where it leaned against the wall.

The familiar smell of male sweat hung in the air, but mixed with something new. The scent of cologne, half sweet, half bitter, faintly familiar.

I went quickly to the corner where James hid, but it was empty. There was no one there. Nothing was disturbed, there was no sign of his presence, but I was sure that someone had been here. I smelt it again, the faint scent of cologne lingering beneath the rotting earthy smells of the barn. A memory stirred in the back of my mind and then receded and I could not recall why it was familiar, where I had smelt it before.

I did not run back to the village, but sat, waiting, crouched back against the wall, bent legs drawn up, hands open. I breathed, long and slow and my mind was as white as the clear sky. In my pocket, I ran my fingers over and over the letter that Magali had given to me.

I sat there for ten minutes, maybe fifteen. But still he did not come.

I started when I heard movement and I was on my feet in an instant. I could not see the door from where I stood, but I was aware that someone was there. I tried not to breathe, my chest constricting with the effort, and for a moment there was a struggle not to call out. For as long as I could remember it had been the other way round: the impossibility of speech, rather than an effort to maintain silence. But there it was, a forgotten impulse, a bodily instinct to expel sound, all but lost, surfacing there in the damp barn as I stood, hardly breathing, listening.

I heard footsteps move slowly across the floor and I pressed myself against the wall, the letter still in my hands, crumpled in my sweating fingers.

I knew the place where he kept his revolver and my hand fumbled for it.

The steps came closer and it was as if they knew about the hiding-place. I drew my breath in sharply as I heard the footfall turn the corner.

It was him.

We faced each other.

I had the revolver in my hand, arms raised, pointing it at him.

It was he who laughed first.

He laughed and I felt my arms shaking, gun still pointed at him. He crossed the remaining distance between us. The gun was still aimed at him, but he folded his hands over it, slowly, carefully.

'You had me worried for a minute there!' he said, his hand on my hand, in which the gun was clasped, the gesture intimate but unfamiliar.

Then, 'I'm sorry if I scared you.' As he took the revolver from me.

For I had not moved, but remained, stiff, back against the wall, the note still in my pocket, hands shaking.

He had tucked the revolver back in its hiding-place and taken a hip-flask from his pocket.

'Here, have some of this. I gave you a shock.'

The flask was pewter, a little bashed, but still shiny. He passed it to me and I took it and lifted it to my lips, tentatively. The smell of the liquid inside was pungent, and I felt it sting my lips even before I swallowed. A bitter taste, mingled with that of the sharp tang of the metal.

I swallowed quickly, the strong liquid rushing to my head, unsteadying me for a moment, making red light spots dance before my eyes.

I passed the flask back to him and he took a swig himself.

'You're cold,' he said.

My body had relaxed a little with the brandy and, as the tautness slipped off, I was caught by trembling.

He was peeling off his jacket and handing it to me. He put it over my shoulders and I could feel the warmth of his body inside it. His hands rested on my shoulders briefly, then he moved away.

'Sit down for a moment,' he said and he dragged out a blanket from the place where it was hidden. Although it was damp, it was not as cold as the bare floor, so I sat on it. He sat next to me and we were side by side, our backs against the wall.

He held the flask in his hands and I noticed now that they were blue from the cold. I took out Magali's letter.

'What's that?' he asked. 'For me?'

I handed it to him. It was wet, the black ink had spread a little but he unfolded it and scanned it quickly.

I watched him, watched the slow smile that spread across his features as he took in its content, watched the way he carefully folded it and put it in his pocket, his fingers running over the crumpled paper, yellow like old skin, touching the words that were written there.

He said nothing about it. Only, 'Thank you.' Then he was silent for a couple of minutes. He appeared to be thinking and he took another swig from the flask.

He passed it back to me and I took another gulp, shivering as I did so, the burning sensation hitting my throat again, searing through me as if it might dissolve my stomach. I felt slightly sick, dizzy, still shivering even beneath his jacket, my head light.

'Will you do something for me?' he asked at last, turning to me. I nodded.

He was scribbling something on the back of Magali's note with the stump of a pencil that he kept in his pocket.

'Can you give this to her for me?' he asked. I nodded.

'It is important,' he said. 'You're sure you'll be able to do it?'

He was looking straight at me, but I could not look back. He seemed, for a moment, totally unfamiliar, like a stranger. I thought of my sister, of the way he held her hands, but I did not say no.

I rose quickly. His jacket had fallen off my

shoulders, but I did not notice. I crossed the barn quickly, feeling a little sick, the new note clutched in my hand. When I reached the door, he called out.

I stopped, turned.

'You'll let me know what she says, won't you?'

I nodded.

He smiled. 'Thank you.'

I turned away, an impression of his smile still in my head. It remained there as I crossed the fields, which were frozen, solid underfoot. I was dizzy with cold and the burning sensation of the brandy.

When I got back to the house it was cold, and empty, and I realized that I had not told him that someone had been in the barn. Nor had I asked him where he had been.

July, 1932

Andrew has been in the village asking questions. I have heard it in the café about the young man who has been to the *mairie*, wanting to look at official records, asking anyone he can find to talk to him about his father, the English soldier who was here during the war.

But he avoids the café. All day I stand by the bar, watching the door, waiting for the little bell above it to ring and to see him step in, dressed in the light English flannels I have seen him wear before. It is summer now, and it is humid, although there has been no sun to speak of yet, just a flat white blanket of clouds that retains the heat below and does not allow the sun to strain through. All day I watch the door, but he does not come.

The old men play boules in the square and I can see them through the window. My father is among them and I watch him as he bends, lifting his arm behind him and then pivots gently into the throw. The ball lands on the ground with a dull thud a few inches from the jack.

My father is a broad man. Older now, but

still strong from carrying barrels and crates from the cellar. Nowadays, increasingly, he allows my sister and me to run the café, while he sits with the other men in the square, packing his pipe with tobacco, watching the smoke rise.

It is late in the afternoon when I see that Andrew has joined them. He is wearing just a shirt and flannels, with the sleeves rolled to the elbow and the collar open. He stands with hands in his pockets, on the edge of the game, watching. A small crowd has started to gather now, the men are returning from the fields and they collect around the game.

Andrew stands amongst them, the young man watching the skill of the old. My father is expert at this game. None of the other men can beat him. He stands up again to play and he is unselfconscious as he takes up a position and holds it, staring forward at the jack. It is, for a moment, as if he were suspended in motion, frozen. Everyone watches as he raises his arm, brings it forward again and sends the orb spinning across the gravel.

From here I cannot see where it goes, but I hear the assembled company clap, and watch my father turn and walk back to where he was standing, the grace of the moment lost and his former awkward gait returned.

The game continues and some of the

young men come into the café to buy glasses of beer which they take out with them. I look up and see that Andrew has moved. He has crossed the square and is standing near my father now. My father watches the game, unaware of the presence of the young man behind him. I see Andrew approach him, offer him a hand.

My father wipes his own on his trousers before proffering it in return. I watch the two men shake hands.

From where I stand, I can hear nothing of their conversation, but I watch their faces: the young man's animated; my father's closed, inscrutable.

It is my father's turn to play again and the crowd is looking to him, but Andrew takes hold of his sleeve as he is about to play. My father turns back, surprised. Andrew is saying something and it angers my father. The game is forgotten now. The two men are about three feet apart and the animosity is evident from the way they stand.

Andrew says something more. My father replies, then Andrew lunges at him, fist raised to strike. A couple of the men who stand nearby step in. Others pull my father away. There is shouting now and raised voices.

I move to the door of the café. My father has walked away from the game, crossing in this direction; Andrew has broken free and he follows him, catches hold of him again, speaks this time in urgent petition.

They are only a few feet away from me now and I can hear him say:

'So why did he stay? Why didn't he escape? Others did. I know it.' My father tries to wrench free of his grip, but does not succeed. 'I've read the reports. There were networks here, safe houses, people who could have smuggled him over the border. Hundreds got away. Why didn't he?' He is no longer shouting now, his anger dissipated. The game is forgotten and the gathered villagers watch the spectacle.

My father does not look at him as he replies:

'We made arrangements.'

'He should have got away.'

'He wanted to stay.' My father pulls away. 'He had his chances to go but he didn't take them. He wanted to stay.' And he tugs himself free of the young man's grip.

He says something else as he moves off which I do not catch but Andrew remains motionless, making no attempt to stop him leaving.

As my father passes me, I touch his arm lightly. He looks down, startled to see me; suddenly he is an old man again. I take his arm and lead him inside. He is solid, like a mule, his movements heavy next to my own, the grace he showed when bowling all gone now.

I look back as I take him inside. Andrew is putting his jacket on, his movements self-conscious. The villagers turn back to the game, but he continues to stare after my father's retreating form.

Claire is standing at the window. She is looking out across the square, where the young man still stands. She lifts her hand to fix a loose strand of hair and I notice that she has tied it back clumsily with string and she is not wearing a ribbon.

The young man moves off and Claire continues to stare after him.

* * *

I walk out to the quarry later because I know that is where he will be.

The weather holds, warm even for this time of year, although there are clouds on the horizon and the old women in the square say that the rain is coming.

You have to go through the copse to get to the quarry. It is maybe quarter of an hour's walk to the north. They used to mine phosphate here and when we were children we used to go to collect the blackberries that grew in abundance, returning home with scratched and berry-stained fingers, our mouths black with gorging on the sweet booty. From the ridge above the quarry, you have a view of the whole region: the green fields of the Pas de Calais laid out before you, as far as Lens and Douai in the north and Cambrai in the south. During the war, you could see the front line from here, and free France beyond it.

He is standing on the ridge, his back to me, hands in his pockets. He is smoking and the way he lifts the cigarette to his mouth in a swift single arc, then holds it there, is exactly as I have seen his father do. I do not move but it seems that he is aware of my presence behind him, in the shadow of the trees, for he says, without even turning:

'Hello there.'

He glances backwards, waiting for my response. I nod. Do not move.

There is silence between us for long minutes. The sun has already gone down but the sky is still white behind grey-blue clouds.

It was at this time of day that I first saw James.

I do not move because this moment seems to mirror the other, to contain something of that long ago day in it. White and blue, past and present, like the streaked, hybrid pattern of the sky.

'You knew my father, didn't you?' he says. He is still facing over the ridge, taking in the view of the fields, stretching to the pock-marked horizon. On a clear day you can see the monument they are erecting at Vimy, the twin pylons of white marble, built to commemorate the Canadian dead, reaching into the sky. He inhales on the cigarette again, a last draw, then throws it down and stubs it out on the ground. I watch his brown-leather shoe grind it into the grass.

'Don't worry. You needn't answer. At least you have an excuse for your silence.' He smiles, an edge of bitterness to his voice.

I remain still, watch the young man look out over the darkening landscape. The light is fading quickly and as his features grow more indistinct it is easier to pretend he is his father.

'I don't remember much about my father, you know,' he says. 'I have a photo of him in uniform, taken just before he left for the front. That's all.'

I hold my cardigan round myself, not cold, but self-conscious.

He has turned a little and I can see his

profile, silhouetted against the streaked sky. His nose is slightly straighter than James's, the cheeks fuller.

'He was very good at football. Played for a local team when he was young.' He digs his hands deep in the pockets of his flannels and kicks the earth with his foot. 'He enjoyed dancing, built radios — he was an expert at that. It was his passion. I remember him trying to show me a few times. But I was too young. I think he was disappointed.' He turns to me. 'People say I look like him.'

I nod at this and he holds my gaze for a second.

'Well, that's something, I suppose.' He smiles, slightly bitter. 'At least I can picture his face.' And there it is again, the odd pull on the vowels that announces his foreignness, despite his excellent command of the language.

He looks back out over the darkening landscape, as if searching for his father where he fell.

'He was decorated, you know.' He is still as he speaks. The colour is slowly draining out of the sky and his outline becomes more blurred. 'The Military Cross: 'For services above and beyond the call of duty', that's what they told us. No more than that.'

He takes out the silver cigarette-case and

removes a cigarette before clicking it shut. He lights the cigarette, cupping the flame with his hands and inhaling quickly. Remembering my presence, he offers me one with a gesture, but I shake my head. It is almost dark now, the sky two shades of indigo and the grass beneath our feet a silky black.

'Services beyond the call of duty,' he half-laughs. 'Doesn't give much away does it?' His hand drops, the orange light of the cigarette making an arc through the blue. He exhales. 'Bit like you, really.' Another half-laugh and a cloud of smoke. Then only the bright orange tip of the cigarette and his dark silhouette against the bruised sky.

'He had a chance to escape,' he says. 'But he came back here. Did you know that?'

I nod.

'I wish I didn't,' he says, not looking at me, but down, at the darkened grass.

I remain still.

After a moment he continues: 'He saw so little active service. What did they award him a medal for, that's what beats me?' He stamps his foot on the ground, a little impatiently.

I uncurl one arm from about my body, leaving the other in place to keep the cardigan round me. I take a step towards him. Stop. Then I reach tentatively for his spare hand. I touch it softly and he looks down, startled by the sudden intimacy, closeness, here in this vast empty space.

His hand is familiar, the shape of the fingers, long nails, smooth palm. I hold it for a moment, studying the pale glowing skin in the darkness before turning it over.

He is watching me, the cigarette forgotten in his other hand. I feel a chill evening breeze prick through my thin cotton blouse to my skin and I shiver.

I do not look at him as I start to trace the pattern on his palm, a pattern I memorized over seventeen years ago.

'Father,' my fingers say, falteringly. 'Love.' The juxtaposition of these two words contains an accidental confession which makes my cheeks burn. Then the final one: 'You.'

I trace the last shape and then let my finger come to a stop, his hand still in mine. I am aware of his breathing in the darkness, the skin on skin, here in the place where his father lay winter after winter.

Andrew does not pull away and I look up to see his eyes, two bright pools in the darkness. For a moment I wonder if I have got it wrong, if he has not understood, if the shapes mean nothing to him after all.

But then he says. 'He taught you.'

I nod.

'My father taught you too?'

And in the darkness, I nod again and then let his hand fall.

December, 1914

It was nearly Christmas, but that year there was none of the usual preparations. Food was scarce and good will was scarcer. Rationing had been imposed with cards and they were rounding up men for forced labour gangs. There were pinched faces in the church to celebrate the advent masses, and the *curé's* message of goodwill to all men pointedly did not extend to the Germans.

A proclamation appeared outside the *mairie*, stating that any allied soldiers hiding in the area who had not yet given themselves up would be regarded as spies and shot. In Le Nouvion, we heard, a young British soldier had handed himself in. After the curfew, when the streets were empty he stepped out on his own into the square, hands above his head. From the windows of the houses, the villagers watched him, a young boy, stepping out into the deserted square, hands above his head. Alone. I was frightenend that James might do this too and so I told him nothing of it.

There were more notes from Magali. They came every couple of days now and James scribbled replies to each and asked me to take them to her. My sister knew nothing of them and I carried them guiltily, like a secret.

There was a pattern now to the handovers. Magali would watch for the times when we children were playing in the square. Then she would come out, wrapped in an old coat of her father's which she now wore. She would stand and watch, smiling, clapping as if she were a child herself. She would watch for five minutes or so, usually. The children liked her, they called out greetings, and she knew each of us by name. When she left, she would make sure she passed where I was standing, and then she would slip a note into my hand, or take one from me. This was how it was done. Often she would squeeze my fingers as she took the paper, the soft pressure like an imprint, or a word on my skin.

I carried the notes to and fro and I watched my sister cross the fields also and return again, treading the same path as mine, knowing nothing about the notes. And I knew that I was betraying her, but I did not stop.

*　*　*

Everyone was talking about the three soldiers they found in Douai, hiding in an attic. Someone had tipped off the Germans, people said. Now the soldiers, one of whom was only nineteen, rumour had it, were to face the firing squad in Peronne. And those who harboured them? They were being sent to prison camps in Germany, the gossips said.

Leutnant Voller confirmed the story one evening after he had eaten. He was looking over some official papers, while my sister cleared the table. It was my father who asked him, breaking his habitual silence to voice the questions that I would have asked if I could.

Voller looked up from the papers he was reading. He seemed pleased by the break in the usually impenetrable silence.

'The British soldiers will be shot, yes,' he confirmed. 'They were found guilty by the court in Peronne.'

'Guilty of what?'

'Of spying.'

'Was there evidence?'

He furrowed his brow. He was looking tired, the gaslight casting translucent shadows on his blond pallor.

'They were given many opportunities to give themselves up. They did not do so.'

'Is that all?'

'As I understand it, yes.'

'But that is not proof that they were spying.' My father seemed exasperated, but not angry yet.

'You have to ask yourself why else they would put good people in danger.'

My father made a clicking noise in his throat. It was a sound I knew, one he made when he was impatient. He stood abruptly and went to put more wood on the fire.

My sister had not moved all this time, but now she looked up and caught Voller's eye for a moment. I saw it. She yielded nothing, looked away again quickly.

'Last week we sent out a company of eight hundred men to the front.' Voller said after a moment. 'Only one hundred and sixty came back. Our leaders are ordering us to push forward, but the British seem to know every time that we are coming. We are sending those men to their deaths. When I write to their mothers, their wives, I need to know that we have done everything we could do for them.'

He stood up, quickly folded his papers and returned them to the inside pocket of his jacket, made a quick bow in the direction of my sister and me.

'I am sorry if I talk out of turn,' he said. 'Please forgive me.' He made his perfunctory excuses and then turned to leave.

At the door he stopped. Turned. His hand was on the latch, in the other he held his hat.

'I am forgetting,' he said. 'The brick

175

outhouse, in the top field, by the copse, it is yours, I think?'

My father nodded. 'Yes, it is.' My sister's face reddened, her eyes darted to the door, but she did not lift her head.

'With regrets, I am forced to ask you to vacate it. The army are requisitioning it for munitions. Please accept my apologies.' He turned again, this time without halting, and went out into the sharp night air. A cold gust swept through the room and then the door slammed and he was gone.

December, 1914

My sister was sick. In the mornings, I saw her throwing up in the corner of the yard where she thought no one could see her. I watched her from the bedroom window, my breath misting the panes, watching the way her body heaved, bent double, the way she spat out bile, retching on nothing, at last leaning against the wall, her breath shallow and fast, her face white, skin damp and clammy, although the earth was still covered in frost which glistened in the sun.

I watched her when she came in, watched the cautious movements she now made around the kitchen, the way her hands fluttered to her stomach as if she were in pain, the way she swallowed over and over again, sometimes just standing still, breathing in heavily until her face regained its colour and her movements took on purpose again.

I watched her and I was frightened. There had been dysentery amongst the soldiers and in the village too. One officer in the bar joked that it took off more of his men than the French and British guns combined that winter. I watched her, and she seemed almost translucent, fragile.

James was restless too. He seemed anxious and he asked mc endless questions: about the new troops which had been arriving; the munitions columns, which way they were heading. He also asked me in a different voice about my sister: about how things were when I was younger; what she liked to do before the war; and about my mother too. He had not spoken like this before and I wanted to ask him how it was that he could speak so softly about my sister but also write the notes to Magali Legrange — almost daily now. I watched his face as he talked and there was a softness there, but also something I did not recognize, the expression I had seen when he looked at the photo of the boy in the sailor-suit, distant, impenetrable. Then I felt I hardly knew him at all.

My fingers told him about the plan to move him.

'Here. Soldiers come. Soon.' I traced one word at a time, slowly, concentrating on each line and shadow.

'Now?' He was alarmed.

I shook my head. 'Soon,' my fingers said.

He had not shaved for days and there was a shadow around his chin that made his skin look grey.

'When?' he asked.

'One week,' my fingers traced. 'Maybe.'

'Damn it!' he said, speaking in English, something he only did when he was agitated. His head was back against the wall, his brows furrowed. He balled his fist and banged out a rhythm on the floor with it, before unfurling his fingers and laying the hand flat.

He lifted his head and looked straight at me.

'Amélie. You have to do something for me.'

I nodded. His face was more serious than I had seen it since the first time I saw him, the time in the woods.

'You and I are friends, aren't we?'

I nodded.

'I have to ask you to do something for me as a friend.' He leant forward and took both my hands in his. His grip was tight, insistent. 'It's very important to me. Can you do it?'

I nodded, unnerved by the urgency in his tone.

'You have to make me a promise.' He kept hold of one hand while the other searched behind a loose piece of brickwork, deliberately loosened to create a small cavity behind. From it, he withdrew an envelope, sealed, the address written in the handwriting I had come to recognize as his.

He put it in my hand and I looked at the sloping writing, unable to make out the letters, running my fingers over the ink, wondering where he had got a pen from. I could make out the last word of the address only and I could see that it said: *England*.

He still had hold of my hand and I looked up, met his gaze.

'You have to promise me,' he said, 'that, if anything happens to me, when the war is over you will post that letter for me. That you will keep it till then. Keep it hidden. Don't show it to anyone. And when the war is over, you'll post it. Will you do that?' He had hold of my hand, tight, his skin hot with the pressure on mine.

I nodded.

'Do you promise?'

I thought of my sister, of the notes I carried to Magali Legrange, of the way Leutnant Voller spoke of the soldiers who were dying in the trenches. I did not know whether to trust him, but the pressure of his hand on mine was almost painful, and his eyes were grey-brown, soft, anxious. I could see myself reflected in them.

And so I took his hand in mine, turned it over, slowly, used my right index finger to trace two words there:

'I promise.'

January, 1915

The café was thick with smoke and the windows were misted with the hot breath of soldiers crammed in there to escape from the cold. The piano in the corner was playing and someone was shouting. Only ten o'clock in the morning, but some men were already drunk and they had the blind, shuttered look of those who had just returned from the front and could not settle until the drink had set in motion the slow process of forgetting.

Henri Marcel was in there too, in the middle of a group of young soldiers, all taller than he. They were laughing and one was slapping him on the back. Marcel was drawing packets of cigarettes out of his coat pockets, like a stage magician. Dutch cigarettes which they were all clamouring to exchange with him for rations; hard sausage, chocolate, loaves of bread wrapped in rags.

I walked past him, ducked behind the bar where my father stood, pulling ale. He was wearing the white apron he always wore, white shirt, black trousers, black tie. White and black, like the tiles on the counter of the bar.

I went into the back and there was my sister, sitting on a chair, head down, panting as if she had been crying. The smell of vomit was thick in the air. She looked up quickly.

'Please. Just go away and leave me alone,' she said.

Her eyes were red and her face pale and I remained still for a moment, unable to move.

'Leave me alone!' She almost shouted it now and it was like a tear, like something ripping. I turned quickly to go and I could hear the soldiers in the bar and, beyond that, the chant from outside in the square, where the children were playing the familiar skipping game, rose in my ears: ' . . . thirty-seven — thirty-eight — thirty-nine . . . '

I ran back to the bar, which was thick now with laughter, Henri Marcel's loud among the rest, shouting something in a crude attempt at German, the alien vowels clotting the air, thick, guttural, like gunshots. He caught sight of me and said something that made them all turn to look at me.

'How's your sister, then?' he asked, in French.

I was in the door to the alcove. They were on the other side of the bar, blocking my way to the exit. My breath was coming quick and shallow and the chant from outside still pounded in my ears.

'She feeling a little queasy in the mornings?' he asked. One of the soldiers translated what he had said and the others laughed, faces towards me, drunken, leering.

I looked about me for another way out, confused.

My father was speaking now. 'Shut up, Marcel. Do you hear me?'

'Come on, Léon! It's not as if people haven't noticed.'

'I said be quiet!' There was a low threat in my father's voice, which made the soldiers laugh nervously.

'She's got a swollen gut like she's eaten a bellyful of eels and a face like toothache — '

'I swear to God, Henri!' My father advanced towards him and the soldiers, sensing a fight, were laughing and pushing Marcel in my father's direction.

'Do you think it'll be blond like him? With those white lashes?' Marcel asked. A quick translation brought forth a new round of laughter.

The words rang in my ears.

'And will it come out speaking in German, do you think, or French? Or perhaps it won't say anything at all, like that one.' He jabbed a thumb in my direction. The laughter had died down and he was speaking directly at my father who was close now, and the antagonism between them was hot and quick.

My brain was racing with the words. The image of my sister inside, the slowness I had seen in her of late. *January, February, March, April, May. How many Kaiser's men did you kill today?*

'Did they do it under your roof, do you think?' Marcel's tone was mocking, unafraid, goading my father who was scarlet with rage. 'At least he's an officer. There's some have done worse.'

My father lunged at him, grabbing him and forcing him against the bar. The German soldiers backed off, stumbling, drunk, laughing, amused at the spectacle.

'You know damn well that's a pack of lies and so do I and if you think you're being clever spreading your filthy rumours then think again because if I hear you've said one more thing about my daughter and that German pig' — he spat out the last word — 'I'll tell them what the hell you've been up to all this time, while you've been playing the jester in here, and I don't care what happens to the rest of us if I do!'

Marcel was panting. He was not a big man and my father's grip had turned his face blue. My father pushed him away roughly and he staggered against the bar, slamming against it with his shoulder. He cried out, but my father just turned away, red-faced, scarcely in control of himself.

He did not hear what Marcel uttered, but I did.

'She's a little whore!' he said, as he gathered himself up, clutching his arm.

The soldiers had lost interest now and returned to their drinks. Marcel was on his own by the bar, a small angry man, like a bullet.

'Just a little whore!'

July, 1932

The late July days are hot, sticky. The yellow light is so bright it seems to be rimmed with black and red and the threat of thunder lies about the heat like an iron lip. It was the same on the day that Claire was born: seventeen years ago today.

I do not see him at first. He stands, just inside the doorway of the café, hat in hand, glancing about him, uncertainly, as if he were looking for somebody.

I am clearing the tables and I notice him only because he stands there for so long without moving that he attracts several glances in his direction which alert me to his presence.

He moves his hat between his fingers. He is wearing a jacket, although it is midsummer and the evenings are still balmy. He looks uncomfortable, hot.

My father is behind the bar, his back to the door, fixing up a new bottle of marc, fiddling with the optic clumsily with arthritic hands. Andrew continues to run the brim of his hat through his fingers.

Eventually he speaks: 'I want to speak to

your daughter, Thérèse,' he says, his voice clear, the English accent pronounced. I wonder for a moment if he has been drinking.

My father does not turn around, just inclines his head. I am surprised that he has not recognized the voice.

'She's out back. Who wants to see her?'

'Andrew Winter,' he says. 'James Winter's son.'

My father stops what he is doing. He turns and surveys the young man by the door slowly. It is a Tuesday night and so the café is nearly empty, but a couple of men sit at a table in the corner and there is another group by the door. They turn to look curiously at the young man with the stiff collar who stands in the middle of the room, staring at my father.

'What do you want with her?' my father asks.

'You know what I've got to say,' Andrew says. He appears nervous, agitated.

'Do I?' My father remains square, stubborn.

'She killed my father.' His eyes are bright. There is a line of perspiration on his top lip.

'My family risked our lives to protect your father.'

'I've been talking to people. I know what happened here.'

'Do you now?'

Claire is standing inside the doorway to the alcove. She is wearing the new dress that my sister has made for her birthday and she has styled her hair differently, in an attempt to look older, although it has the opposite effect. I do not know if she has heard what Andrew has said.

My sister appears from behind her and it is her presence which draws his eyes to the doorway, for he has not noticed Claire. Mother and daughter are framed in the arch of the alcove. Two faces, one an uneasy replica of the other, the cheeks fuller, the lights softer, less starkly differentiated from the shade. Only the eyes are different, as if they had been painted from another palette.

My sister has seen him and as she does so her hand goes out instinctively to her daughter's shoulder. Claire looks up, momentarily startled by her touch.

'Do you want to speak to me?' my sister says.

'Yes,' he stumbles. 'Yes, I do.' He seems more diffident now, in her presence, his fervour abated. 'I want you to tell me why you did it.'

'What did I do?' she asks, hand still on Claire's shoulder, as if for support.

'You told the Germans where my father

was hiding.' He looks red-faced, determined.

'Who told you that?' she says.

'I have spoken to a lot of people. Here in the village, elsewhere.'

'I'm sure you have.' She smiles wryly. 'And what did they tell you?'

'Your family was never arrested. Everyone else who knew about him was arrested, sent to prison camps in Germany, fined, but they never came for you.'

My sister does not answer.

'It was your barn he was hiding in. Why wouldn't they take you?'

'He was found out by the quarry,' says my sister, quiet, not looking at him now, but looking down at Claire, stroking her hair. 'He wasn't in our barn when they took him.'

Claire is caught between them, not knowing where to look.

'You are a beautiful woman.' He colours as he says this, looks down at his hands then back at her again quickly. 'They say your family never went short of anything.'

She colours. 'I'm sure they say a lot more than that about me,' she says, defiant, angry, with the look in her eyes I have seen there before when things have been said, in here, about Claire, about my sister, drunken things, cruel things, crudely spoken.

'I know about your daughter too. About the

name on her birth certificate.'

Claire starts and reddens.

'She has my name on her birth certificate,' my sister answers. Her eyes scan the room. The men sitting at tables have paused in their conversations and are listening, enjoying the spectacle. 'There's plenty of others in this village have the same, if truth be told.'

Claire looks down, red-faced, confused. Her hair has been clumsily pinned at the back and it is already starting to come apart, small tendrils falling over the nape of her neck.

'Were you in love with my father?' Andrew asks, and when my sister does not answer, he repeats the question: 'Were you in love with him?'

For a moment, I think my sister is going to laugh. Mirth rises in her eyes but she says nothing.

'Were you?'

Still nothing.

'Do you know what I think,' he says. 'I think you wanted him and he wouldn't have you.'

She half-smiles but does not look away.

'He told you he had a wife and family at home, that he loved my mother, that he would not betray her. Would not betray us.'

My sister looks at him, her brow furrowed, the faint smile still playing about her lips. He stares back defiantly but it is easy to see the fear that lies behind his emphatic assertion. He looks just like his father.

'You're right,' she says, 'He loved you. He loved your mother. He would never have done anything to hurt either of you. He loved you very much.' I know what it has cost her to say this and I know too that, in its own way, it is true.

Claire looks up at her, just once, and only briefly, then looks away.

'Why did you do it,' he says, after a moment. 'Can you just tell me that?'

I think that he must hear my breathing, which comes thick and fast now, that he will turn to see me, standing in the corner, cloth in hand, tearless, silent. I wait for her denial, but all she says is:

'I loved him.'

He looks crushed by this, hurt, as if she had let him down in some inexplicable way. Lost, like someone who has reached his destination after long journeying only to find there is nothing there and that he has forgotten what he came for. He looks down to the hat in his hands, his face red.

'Thank you,' he says. He does not move but continues to stare at his hands. He has nothing more to say. His anger is spent but he has nowhere to go and it is as if he has just realized this. 'Thank you,' he says again, then moves towards the door, which yields to his touch with a high tinkling of the little bell.

It is dark outside now and he steps out into it. I want to run after him, stop him, fill the space between us with words. But I do not.

And it is Claire whom I see looking out after his retreating form, and it is she, after all, who has lost most with this departure. I see my sister lift a hand to straighten the hair that has fallen loose at the nape of her daughter's neck, but Claire appears not to notice. She stares out towards the door that he walked through and shrugs my sister's hand away.

January, 1915

Magali Legrange wore a man's coat wrapped around her slim frame. She had grown more slender since the outset of the war, gaunt almost. She crossed the square quickly. I watched her movement, the thin legs in heavy shoes, the shapeless coat hugged about her, fleshless hands blue with the cold. Her head was uncovered and the coppery curls of her hair were exposed above her delicate features, lending them a vitality which usually they lacked. She was not beautiful as my sister was beautiful but the freezing weather made her eyes bright and her skin glow.

She stood for some time watching the game. It was my turn to skip. I jumped in, the long rope whipping past my ankles, clearing my feet just on time, lifting them higher and higher with each turn of the rope. I could hear the others chanting, the old song, it had become a favourite now and we had forgotten that there was ever another:

January, February, March, April, May.
How many Kaiser's men did you kill
today?

And then jumping: *One — two — three — four* . . . I could see the cloud my own breath made as I jumped over and over, and through it the figures of the children who clustered around the one who was turning a rope, Marie Berniers, her hair a smudge against the snow, her face pink, leaping, distorted as the rope whipped past it, faster and faster. I thought of my sister, red-faced, shouting at me to leave her alone.

And I was aware of Magali Legrange, watching. The counting got louder as I jumped faster and faster and higher and higher and I could hear her voice which had joined in with the rest, low beneath the childish pitch of the others. I could no longer keep up with the shapes the numbers made in the air, all I could think of was to keep jumping, not to let the flying rope catch my heels.

The panic that had lain low in me for days rose quick and fast now in my panting breaths and I felt as if I must keep jumping to ward off what was coming, so I kept it up, lifting my legs again and again, chest screaming, tight: *eighty-seven — eighty-eight — eighty-nine* . . . more than anyone had ever done before, *ninety-three — ninety-four* . . . On and on I jumped, always aware of Magali Legrange clapping, counting with the others, a letter for James in her pocket, while my sister sat, panting through sickness in the back room.

One hundred and two — one hundred and three . . . Still the rope swung and still I jumped. Through the dim mist of blind breathlessness I was aware of another figure appearing at Magali's side, drawing her off, so that her voice was no longer audible among the shouts which chronicled my epic triumph. I could just make out another figure taking her aside, talking to her urgently. A man, dark-haired, I could not make out his features, but I caught on the breeze the merest scent of cologne, musky familiar. He pulled her off across the square and I turned my head to try and catch a proper look at his face.

In that moment of turning my foot twisted and the rope caught on my leg. I felt myself descend, felt a sharp pain in my ankle as I fell heavily. The rope was twisted about me and I was breathless, head black with the exertion, blood pounding in my ears so that the excitement of the others who crowded around me was magnified, distorted, echoing and drumming in my head as through a churning sell of water. They clustered around excited, for it was the longest anyone had jumped, a new record in the square, and now everyone was clamouring to be the next, to have a go at beating me.

But I was not listening to them. I was trying to get up, to get through them, to get away from Magli Legrange. I did not want to carry another note. A sour taste was in my mouth, bitter like the bile I had seen my sister choking on this morning.

But Magali was not looking in this direction, but staring off towards the road, where the man must have gone, her hands no longer hugging her coat about her, but hanging by her sides, exposed to the chill wind.

She turned, caught sight of me. Behind me, they were squabbling about who should jump next. I tried to move off but she was quicker than me and she caught hold of my arm.

'You remind me of your sister. She could jump just like that,' she said and I flushed, aware of her hand on my arm. I could feel that beneath her laughter she was trembling and there was a new note of urgency in her voice which was at odds with the bright smile. The game had resumed, and the chanting started up again.

'You can talk to him, can't you.' She whispered hurriedly. I did not respond. 'He told me you could.' I remained still, so she went on: 'Can you give him a message?' she asked. 'It's urgent. I don't have time to write another note.'

I glanced quickly in the direction of the café, desperate to get away.

'Please,' she said, her tone imploring.

I glanced again at the café. I hesitated a moment, feeling tears rise hot to my eyes. Then I nodded.

'Thank you,' she said, the relief palpable in her voice. 'Tell him . . . tell him plans have changed. Tell him it must be tonight. Not when the note says. Tonight. Can you do that?' She bent down in front of me, looked at me closely, her eyes darting quickly to the other side of the square where a cluster of German soldiers were gathered. 'It must be tonight.'

I nodded, unnerved by the low note of alarm discernible in her voice.

'And give him this.' She pressed a note quickly into my hand, straightening as she did it so that the gesture looked innocuous. 'But tell him it must be tonight.'

She smiled, although her eyes were anxious. 'Just like your sister,' she said and then she turned away, pulling the coat about her slim frame.

The chant had started up again:

January, February, March, April, May.
How many Kaiser's men did you kill
 today?
One — two — three — four . . .

I ran back to the house, the note clutched in my hand. I wanted to throw it away, to burn it.

Just inside the kitchen, I stopped. My sister was standing by the fireplace and she turned as I came in. She saw me stop, red-faced, the letter in my hand.

I shoved it hastily into my pocket, but she had already caught sight of it.

'What have you got?' she said. She took a couple of steps towards me. 'A note? Is it from James?' There was anxiety in her tone now. Her face was still pale, taut, drawn.

My fingers tightened around the slip of paper.

'What is it? Show it to me.'

I took a step backwards.

'Come on. Show it to me.' She reached towards my pocket and I pulled away, but she grabbed my hand, wrested the note out of it. Her hands were warm, coarse from her endless duties about the house and café: an old woman's hands on a young girl.

I watched her as she tore it open. She read it slowly, although it was short, only a few lines. I watched her redden, saw her breath quicken. She turned away slightly, her hand dropping to her side. I waited for her to speak, but she said nothing.

I wanted to reach out and touch her, run my fingers over the rough skin of her palms.

'Who gave you this?' she asked after a moment.

I was silent.

She turned to look at me. She did not often look straight at me, and I was unnerved by her gaze.

'I don't suppose you would tell me, even if you could.' She looked at me a moment longer, then turned away. She sighed. 'I'm not sure I really want to know.'

She moved over to the table and lowered herself slowly into a chair.

'I suppose you've known all along,' she said.

I wanted to shake my head, tell her it was not true, but I could not.

She put the note down on the table and pushed it towards me.

'Go on, you'd better take it.'

I hesitated, uncertain what to do.

'Take it. It sounds important. Take it.'

Confused, I stepped forward, picked up the note without looking at her. I turned and left the house quickly, an image of her face stinging in my brain as I went back out to the square where the snow had started to fall in soft flakes. The children had scattered now. I stood alone on the cobbles, the letter in my hand, no longer making any attempt to hide it.

January 1915

James was just sitting there and I think that as soon as I saw him, I knew it was for the last time.

It was snowing heavily outside and it was cold in the barn. It was the first time that I noticed the permanent state of cold and damp in which he had lived throughout the winter. He looked dirty that day, unshaven and I saw that his clothes were grimy. He smiled when he saw me, as he always did, although I had no food for him, nothing.

'Hello,' he said. 'Nice to see you. Are you well?'

I nodded quickly, shivering, but not with the cold.

I passed him the note and he read it, then I took his hand, making as little contact as possible with his skin, quickly spelt out Magali's message in urgent strokes.

'Tonight?' he said. He looked at me. 'Are you sure?'

I nodded.

'You're sure she said tonight. Not tomorrow?' He seemed anxious.

I wanted to tell him what she said. That

plans had changed. That it had to be tonight. But I only had one word to do it. 'Change,' my fingers said. And then again, 'Tonight.'

He nodded, then looked away, lost in thought.

An image of my sister bloomed in my head and I felt dizzy, sick, confused.

'Listen,' he said, suddenly. 'I have to go away for a bit.'

I nodded.

'I'll try and get back soon.'

I listened to him, my hands cold at my sides.

'Tell your sister . . . ' he halted, a pained expression on his face, 'tell her I'll be back. That I haven't gone for good.' He stopped again, remembering. He half-laughed then, more to himself than to me. 'But you can't do that for me, can you? Of course you can't.'

He buried his head in his hands for moment, still laughing lightly, although there was no joy in the sound. I leant forward quickly and took one of his hands. He looked up.

'You — love — her?' my fingers asked.

'Do I love your sister?' He looked straight at me now and I felt my stomach tighten, bubbles of fear rising up in me. 'Yes, I do,' he said. 'Although, God knows I tried not to.'

I felt the tears welling now. The hot liquid

rose to my eyes and I struggled to keep it back. I didn't know what else to ask. I felt as if I knew the rest. I did not want to ask him about Magali Legrange, about the notes, did not want to know any more.

'You should go,' he said. 'You don't want them to find you here.'

But there was one more thing. He was rising, but I grasped at his hand.

'How — you — learn,' I stopped, lacking the words to ask what I wanted. Then: 'Talk — fingers.'

'How did I learn to talk with my fingers?' he said. His face was swimming for my eyes were full of tears and my face ached, taut with the effort of holding them back. 'I wondered when you were going to ask me that.' He stopped, looked at me, his brow creased. Then he crouched down again so that his face was level with mine. 'My wife is deaf,' he said. He said it clearly, slowly, four little words echoing against the ache of tears in my head.

I was frozen.

'I am married,' he said, continuing in the same clear, slow voice. 'And I have a son. I learned sign language when I met my wife. So that I could talk with her.'

I rose to unsteady feet, the tears had stopped now. They were trapped again, like the words were, trapped deep.

'I didn't intend to fall in love with your sister. I tried to leave, to stop it, but . . . ' he broke off her . . . 'I had to come back.'

But I was looking away now. He had my hand in his, but my face was turned away from him. He waited a moment, but I did not turn back.

He rose and touched my cheek with his hand and it felt cold next to my hot skin.

'I hope I haven't hurt you,' he said. 'I never meant to.' Then, 'The letter I gave you. It is for my son. When the war is over, will you post it for me?'

I did not turn to face him, but I nodded to say that I would, then I wrenched myself from the touch of his fingers on my cheek and ran out of the barn, back out into the snow.

★ ★ ★

Leutnant Voller was sitting there, at the table, smoking, scouring a map, in his shirt-sleeves, although the snow swirled thick in the air outside. He was the only one in the house. He looked up when I came in the back door, nodded. Perhaps if he had not been there I would not have done it.

'Hello,' he said, looking up only briefly before returning his eyes to the map.

I just stood there, breathless from running, clogged with words that I wanted to say.

There were sounds, backed up in my throat, making my breaths come more quickly, unevenly. My mouth opened, closed, my lips parted and I swallowed with the effort, but nothing came. I bit my lip hard, tears rising hot to my eyes.

I tried again and this time I managed to mouth the words but still no sound came out, my tongue felt dull, heavy. I shaped the sentence once more with my lips as I had learned to do with my fingers.

James always said that if I could talk with my hands I could do it with my lips too. He always said it was the first step. I thought of his face again, his expression as he said: *I have a wife and a child.*

I closed my eyes, swallowing again with the effort. This time, painfully, slowly, I forced out a sound from somewhere in my gut.

It sounded odd, not as I heard myself in my head, but closer, ringing in my ears, thick, lisping, dull with the weight of a lazy, untrained tongue.

The sound broke the silence and Voller looked up, quickly. I tried again, tears overtaking me now, making the sound more clouded still.

'Soldier.' I heard myself saying. It was my

first word and I released it with a sob.

'Good God, what are you saying?'

'English.' Thick with tears.

Then, with the greatest effort of all. 'Barn.'

The silence had been broken, and I felt as if something had been ripped out of me, as if I might bleed and bleed from this torn place and never stop.

He was standing, pushing back the chair.

'What are you saying?'

He took a step forward and I backed away, frightened suddenly, not wanting to hear my own voice again, scared of the words I had already spoken.

So I turned and ran, leaving my words in the room, irretrievable, indelible.

He called out after me, but I did not look back.

January, 1915

The next day the bombardment started before sunrise. The Germans had been shelling the British line for days, but that night the shells fell silent. At dawn the mist crept over no man's land, over the corpses that were indistinguishable from one another now in the snow: German and British briefly communing in shared burial beneath the banks of white. At around six the mines went off, a succession of earth-shattering explosions, the reverberations of which were felt for miles.

Lying beside my sister, listening to the soft ebb and flow of her breathing, I felt the first tremor. She stirred briefly in her sleep, flung an arm over me. As the explosions continued, I lay still, unmoving, hardly breathing, feeling the weight of her arm upon me. Then, after twenty minutes, came the attack and the air was rent with sound: the monstrous rattle of the guns; the wailing screams of the smaller shells; the inhuman cries of the wounded. Clear, caught on the wind, I heard them, the unnatural wails of men.

The snow started to fall again mid-morning. A flurry of white that seemed to tug new currents of cold out of the air. My sister and I cleaned the café, for it was empty that day.

Out in the square I saw truckloads of cheap pine boxes which they were taking down towards the front. Made of bright yellow wood, hastily thrown together, it was with a shock that I realized that they were coffins. Truck-load after truck-load of them went past, hundreds of crude pine beds for the boys at the front to rest in that night.

My sister and I worked in the café: she with a scarf wrapped around her head, both of us with our sleeves rolled up to the elbow. Together, we lifted the chairs on to the tables, with their legs facing upwards, together we scrubbed as if we might clean away the sound of death and carnage in the air. The floor was grimy where the mud and snow had been tramped in on soldiers' boots, and the walls were greasy with handprints.

The sound of fighting had settled into a pattern now and we moved silently amongst the tables, weaving about each other, as if dancing to the imperceptible rhythm of the artillery.

Beneath her breath, she was humming, and occasionally a snatch was audible. I recognized the tune. It was one my mother used to sing. There was water on the floorboards, staining them dark where her mop had been.

The door opened and I turned, half-expecting to see Voller again. But it was not Voller; it was Henri Marcel. He wore heavy boots and they were caked in mud.

My sister stopped what she was doing and looked up, expectant. My heart was beating fast. Marcel walked straight across the wet floor, his muddy footprints showing chalky against the dark, soaked wood.

'Cognac,' he said, dragging one of the upturned chairs from a table and sitting down.

My sister went behind the bar, got him a cognac, placed it on the table in front of him.

'What's happened.'

He downed the drink in one.

'They found a soldier in the woods.'

I saw my sister start. Her eyes were bright, the Cognac bottle suddenly loose in her hand.

'Where?'

'Didn't say.'

'Is it . . . ?' She faltered. 'Is it him?'

'Dunno.' He sniffed, saw me, standing across the other side of the room, now motionless, staring. 'Reckon she knows though.' He nodded in my direction. I reddened.

'Amélie hasn't been there today.'

'Found him yesterday, they reckon,' Marcel replied.

My sister turned towards where I stood, motionless. I was aware of the blood rushing to my face, the panic of tears rising. She moved quickly, clutched me by the shoulders. Her touch was sudden, violent, unexpected, her fingers hot through the rough fabric of my blouse.

'Did you see him last night? Was he there?'

I said nothing.

She shook me, eyes vacant with panic.

'Was he there?'

My body felt loose, like a doll's beneath her grasp. I shook my head. Just once.

Her grip loosened and she stepped back, a couple of steps, on to the wet floor. Stranded there, cut off.

Henri Marcel hadn't moved from where he sat, watching her.

'What did they do to him?' My sister was staring ahead, her hand on her belly, scarcely conscious either of us was there.

'I heard he was shot.'

I saw her start, as if an invisible bullet had

caught her from behind.

'He tried to escape. They gunned him down.'

My sister turned away, moved towards the table nearest the door, reaching out for one of the upturned chairs to hold on to, tightening her grip around the wooden leg to support herself.

'Someone tipped them off,' Marcel was saying. 'Someone who knew he was there, that's what they're saying.'

She didn't turn around. Her reflection was caught in the mirror on the far side of the café, the shapes of her grief trapped within the green-and-gold lettering.

'Please,' she said, speaking to the reflection. 'Please leave us alone.'

He stood up, turned to go, pulling his cap roughly over his head as he stepped once more on to the damp floorboards. He stopped beside my sister.

'You want to tell your father what's happened. There's trouble for us all in this.' Then he glanced at me as he said: 'Unless you've made your own private arrangements, that is.'

He held my gaze for a moment and I reddened under it.

He went after that and it was just Thérèse and me, left alone in the bar, steam from the wet floor clouding the windows. She stared at her face in the mirror, her gaze unswerving, her body rigid, hands white.

I went over, tentative steps, until I was right beside her, but she did not seem to notice. I was nearly as tall as her by then. I could see the little curls of hair escaping from the scarf at the nape of her neck, baby hairs, soft, downy against the white skin. She was trembling.

I reached a hand to touch one of hers. She flinched but I continued. Her hand was cold, smaller than my own. I folded my palm over hers, teased open the taut fingers.

Her hands were rough, the skin chapped, dragging against my own. I took one, turned it over, ran my fingers over it, caressing the grooves. I traced a pattern, once, twice, three times. Looking at her all the time.

She did not move. Did not look at me.

I lifted my other hand to her face, stroked my fingers across her brow, where the baby-hairs escaped.

I do not know how long we stood like that, silent, still but for the motion of my fingers, for it was a long time before she started to cry.

★ ★ ★

Voller returned mid-morning. I saw him arrive in an army staff-car, driven by a soldier in a peaked cap who saluted him as he got out. I watched him cross the square. His greatcoat and hat were covered in dark patches where the snow had soaked through. He walked quickly, head down against the blizzard, pushed open the door roughly so that the bell set off a frantic high-pitched ringing.

I was alone in the café now. He did not see me at first. He pulled off his hat, still ridged with snow, stamped his feet, looked around for my father. His face was set in an expression I had not seen on him before. The same look I had seen in the men who returned from the front. Opaque. He looked around for my father. I felt certain that he had come to arrest him.

Then he saw me, sitting at the table by the window. He asked simply:

'Where's your father?'

I pointed in the direction of the cellar.

He nodded assent, started to move. Stopped.

He was three or four feet away. His blond hair was damp, flattened by the hat, which had made an impression like a red bevel across his forehead.

'Your soldier's gone.'

I said nothing. Conscious of the cold glass behind my back, the moisture from his jacket dripping on the floorboards, I nodded my head. My father had appeared in the doorway to the cellar. Voller saw him. I watched him approach my father, my heart pounding.

But all he said was: 'We need all the spirits you have. They need it in the dressing stations.' His tone was curt, demanding, the chivalrous politeness all gone out of it, but with no hint of aggression. 'I'm sending some men to come and collect it.'

My father was about to protest, but Voller was scarcely looking at him. His face was red.

'They are dying like pigs out there. The least we can do is give them some liquor to numb the pain.'

He turned and went out quickly, pushing the door roughly open and allowing it to slam as he went out. I watched as he climbed back into the waiting vehicle which reversed quickly and sped off out of the square.

August, 1932

Magali Legrange is sitting at the kitchen table. She has not taken her coat off and she holds her handbag on her knee. Her gloves sit in front of her, the slope of her hands still evident in the fabric, but shrunken now, deflated.

My sister stands by the sink, her back to Magali, stationary.

Both women look round when I come in.

Magali smiles. 'Amélie,' she says, her voice warm.

I move my head in an answering nod.

'It's nice to see you,' she says.

I take off my coat and hat and hang both on the hook behind the door.

'I am sorry to arrive like this, unannounced,' she says. 'Perhaps I should have told you I was coming.' She looks over to me. My sister still hasn't spoken. I do not sit down. 'I hardly recognized you, Amélie,' she continues.

'What do you want?' My sister does not turn to her as she says this, but it is not said in anger either. She looks tired. Her hair is carelessly done.

Magali glances at her, does not reply straight away.

'I always thought you did it,' she says. 'Though I never really understood why.' She pauses. 'You loved James, didn't you.'

My sister shrugs, her face closed.

I remain where I am, on the other side of the room.

'Did you know he was married?' she asks my sister.

'Are you reproaching me for it?' Thérèse half-turns towards her.

'No.' Magali pauses. 'No, I'm not. Do you mind if I smoke?'

My sister shakes her head and Magali reaches into her handbag and takes a cigarette out of a half-empty packet. She offers them to us both, but my sister shakes her head and I look away, so she replaces the pack in the small, neat handbag and takes out a woman's lighter in leather casing. I notice as she does so that her fingers are unsteady, her nails painted. She used not to paint her nails. She has a sophistication now that my sister lacks, something of the town about her, although she wears it awkwardly, like an ill-fitting dress.

There is silence as Magali returns the lighter to her bag.

'How is Claire?' she asks.

'She's well.'

'Is she like him?' Magali lifts the cigarette to her lips, inhales quickly, exhales slowly.

My sister looks over at me, shrugs. I nod.

'He'd be proud of her,' Magali says.

My sister says nothing.

Magali looks from me to her. 'Andrew Winter came to see me.'

'He came here too,' Thérèse replies.

'He is so like his father, I . . . ' she stops and for the first time I wonder why she never married, whether there has ever been anyone for her. 'He told me a little about his mother.'

I see my sister stiffen.

'She was engaged to James's brother, did you know that?' My sister says nothing. 'But he died. A riding accident, I think. She was an old friend of the family.' She pauses, and I wonder if my sister knew this. Her face indicates nothing. 'James married her in his brother's place. That's how Andrew tells it.'

Magali inhales again on the cigarette, waiting for a response from my sister, but there is none. 'You probably knew that,' she says, after a moment.

Still no response from Thérèse.

'He said they found James's body by the quarry. Is that true?' Magali says after a moment.

My sister nods.

'I hadn't realized.' Magali holds her cigarette uncomfortably. It does not suit her, smoking, and she does it without grace. I realize that she is nervous. She has not been here in over seventeen years: she never came back after the war. 'I always thought they found him in your barn. I wondered why they didn't make his execution more public.'

She seems lost in thought for a moment. She is trying to say something but appears not to know how to come at it. Eventually, she says: 'James was good at radios. You probably knew that also.' I watch the cigarette: the thin line of smoke, the slow diminishment of the paper-white tube. 'There was some equipment. They had to abandon it in the retreat. James gave the order. It was left at the quarry.'

My sister stares out of the window.

'Did you know that he was sending messages back across the lines, to the British HQ?' Magali asks.

I can see from the expression on my sister's face that this is news to her.

Magali goes on. 'I think at first he was just looking for a way to escape. Hoped they could help him. He asked them to let his family know he was safe. I think he got a couple of mesages back to them.' She is looking at my sister, who flinches almost imperceptibly at this reference to his English family. 'But British Intelligence realized he could be valuable.'

There is a pause.

'How do you know this?' my sister asks, turning now to face her.

Magali hesitates. Sighs. 'There was a network. Organizing resistance activities on a small scale. Pamphlets, smuggling out British and French soldiers, and local men of serviceable age who were liable to be taken for forced labour.' The cigarette is nearly all burned out now, the glowing tip almost touching the brown-paper filter. 'At first, I just got involved in helping James to escape.'

She lifts the near-dead cigarette to her lips and takes a last drag, then looks about for somewhere to stub it out. My sister takes a saucer from the dresser and passes it to her. For a moment, the two women look at one other and then my sister looks away, rubs her hands on her apron, and returns to her earlier position, arms crossed against her chest now.

'Only, of course, he didn't want to.' Magali smiles, extinguishes the cigarette. 'He came back for you, you know. He could have got out, gone home. Someone else could have done what he did. He chose to stay.'

My sister uncrosses her arms, certainties of the past unsteadied, muddied.

Magali goes on: 'The network gathered information on troop movements. James's role was to pass it on to British HQ. It alerted them to when the Germans were going to push forward, so they were prepared.' She looks at my sister then at me.

I have remained unmoving by the door. I am thinking of the notes. On scraps of paper, carried in my pocket across the field.

'Who else knew this? Apart from you?' my sister asks.

'In our village?'

My sister nods.

'My father knew a little. Then just Henri Marcel and myself. Henri hung around the German barracks, sold the soldiers cigarettes, played the clown. He gathered a lot of information that way.' She stops again, hands on the table, aimless now without the cigarette. She picks up one of her gloves, plays with it. 'He was in his element. He used to go and see James, tell him what he knew, take him books. It was foolish — he might have been seen.' Memory shifts and I recall the scent of cologne, familiar, lingering in the barn. 'I wasn't so brave. I sent information by the notes that Amélie took.'

She looks at me now. 'I am sorry to have used you like that, not to have explained. I shouldn't have got you involved.'

220

Still I cannot look at her. I shrug and look away, feeling the hot rush behind my eyes that threatens tears.

'How did he do it?' My sister says this and Magali turns away from me, towards her. 'How did he send the messages?'

'He used the radio equipment that had been left at the quarry. He had a length of wire and he rigged it up to a tree on the high ground. It was pretty crude, but it worked. The big German offensive in January of 1915, the British knew it was going to happen. They were ready. He saved a lot of lives by what he did, you know.'

My sister nods, says nothing for some time.

'I always thought it was you,' she says eventually.

I am on the other side of the room separated by a distance of three or four feet. Neither woman looks at me.

'I know you did.' Magali smiles at my sister, a thread of understanding strung out between them.

'He wasn't supposed to have been at the quarry,' Magali says, 'Not that night. There were certain times when it was clear for him to go. But plans changed at the last minute. When Andrew told me that's where they found him, I suddenly realized.'

My breaths come quick, shallow now as a

dim realization forms, half-clouded, and I stumble towards it. *Thirteen — fourteen — fifteen — sixteen* . . . jumping in the square, clouded breath, Magali clapping with the rest, a figure approaching her.

'I looked at the official papers,' Magali says. 'They arrested everyone in the network over the few weeks after James disappeared, you know. We were all sent to prison camps in Germany. I wondered sometimes if it was James who told them. I think that's what they wanted us to believe. That's why they didn't give him a trial, just allowed him to disappear. To make us doubt him. But I could never bring myself to believe it.'

I have turned away while she has been speaking, my face towards the fireplace, hand on the mantelpiece to steady myself.

'There was only one person who could have told them that he was at the quarry that night,' Magali says. I do not turn, but I twist my mouth to shape the name that is in my mind. Four syllables, a figure disappearing across the square: dark hair, a squat frame, the scent of cologne.

Behind me I hear Magali sound out the same syllables: 'Henri Marcel!'

A chill breeze that stings like relief lifts somewhere in my mind. I realize that I am shaking.

'But they arrested Henri Marcel,' I hear my sister say. I look at her, only half-recognizing her. 'Why would they do that if it was him?'

'I looked at the court records in Peronne,' Magali says. 'He was fined and sentenced to prison in Germany, but it was rescinded. He went to Germany for a bit, but he never served a sentence.'

My sister is silent for a moment, still, not angry, as if all the rage has been washed out of her. Then she asks the question that I know she will ask:

'Why didn't they arrest my family?'

'I don't know,' says Magali and both women are still. 'Perhaps only you know the answer to that.'

And the two women look at each other and neither looks at me. And words flap at my breast like dark wings, and I want to shout and break the silence of seventeen years, but I do not.

Eventually, my sister moves, a little heaviness in her gait now, betraying the fact that nearly two decades have passed.

'I am going to make us some tea,' she says. 'Would you like some?'

January, 1915

It was quiet the night they found James, as was so often the case the night before a big push. The eerie silence of fear pulsed in waves from the soldiers who crouched in trenches, waiting for the order at dawn. The barracks were empty. The Germans had sent all available men down to the front. The night was beautiful, freezing, full of fear.

It was getting dark when I ran out of the house, the bitter taste of my first words choking me, like petals stuffed in my throat. I could hear Voller calling after me, but I did not look back, only ran, knowing that I must get to James before he did, knowing that words spoken cannot be unspoken, that the safety of silence, once shattered, can never be regained. And the snow had already formed a coating on the ground, so that my feet left tracks in the fields as I stumbled on towards the copse, desperate now, falling, cracking my knee, feeling the damp blood ooze out of it, but hardly noticing the pain, only wanting more words now to erase those I had spoken.

When I reached the barn I stopped. I stood in the doorway, the dark not clearing to reveal any more than a repetition of itself. Panting, my chest heaving, I had no breath to form speech at first. His name came out like a cry, like the word I had been holding on to all along. 'James!' I called, but there was no response. I called again and again, my words audible: real words, spoken aloud, but useless now, since there was no one there to hear them.

For he had already gone.

July, 1932

I take the letter out of the drawer and turn it over in my hand. It has lain there for seventeen years and the paper is now yellowing, the ink faded to a dull brown, but the handwriting is still familiar.

I sit on the end of the bed, the envelope in my hand. I can see myself in the mirror in the corner of the room. I see a young woman with a face not unlike my sister's. The hair is a little darker, the nose less pronounced, the lips not so full, but the eyes are the same. I am a few years older than she was when James came, and it shows in the slight lines around my mouth and forehead. But the eyes are the same.

I look away from my reflection, back to the letter. I touch the flap, which is loose now; the gum has dried over the years. I allow my fingers to slide under the seal. It lifts easily. I take out the folded sheets inside, two of them, densely written on both sides in his characteristic, looping style.

The letter is written in English, so the words mean nothing to me. I run my fingers over them, but they yield no meaning to my touch.

I hear footsteps behind me and turn to see Claire standing in the doorway. She smiles and I motion for her to come and sit beside me. She comes in and loops an arm about my waist. I look at her, lift a hand to her face, and I think, not for the first time, that anything I might have wanted from James has been granted to me in her.

'What's that?' she asks, motioning to the letter in my hand.

I hesitate for a moment. I know that she will be able to read it; she is learning English at the Lycée in Cambrai. Sometimes in the evenings she sits and reads her lessons aloud and I am reminded of James in her crude English inflexions. I pass the letter to her.

She takes it from me and pauses as she glances at it. 'It's from him, isn't it?' she says, after a moment.

I nod.

She says nothing, but unfolds the faded sheets carefully. I watch her as her eyes scan the words he has written there. When she is finished, she looks away and says nothing.

After a few moments she says, 'Do you want me to read it to you?' Her voice is steady, but her cheeks are pale and she does not look at me.

I nod and she starts to read.

My dear Andrew,
I cannot imagine when or whether this letter will reach you. Time only will tell, but I pray that somehow, by some good chance, it might.

I wonder if you will still remember me, and whether you have forgiven me yet for leaving you to go away to war.

You will have learned by now that I am missing. I was injured in late August 1914, and I lost my regiment in the retreat. Since then I have been cared for compassionately by good people. They have looked after me with Christian kindness, not heeding their own safety. I have come to love them.

She stops here, her voice unsteady, puts down the sheet. His words breathe in the corners of the room, imminent. She picks up the sheet of paper again and resumes.

I have met someone here who has taught me the value of words and of the need to say the things you feel and not remain silent. So, I have to tell you that I have thought of you every day, that I have wanted to be at home to do all the things a father should do with his son: take you fishing, teach you to box. My greatest regret is that I have missed so much of your childhood, and that I might never live to see you grow into a man.

However, I have served my country in the way that was available to me. Returning was not an option. I have done my duty and hope that in so doing I may have saved the lives of others, even if it is to cost me my own. For the sake of those who have helped me here, whom I have come to love and respect, I can say no more, and my only hope is that I will not pay the price for this with your misunderstanding as well as with my life. I trust that one day you will learn what I have done here and you will understand why I was unable to return.

I have only one thing with which to reproach myself. I regret that I must tell you in this way, but it is something you must know. There is a girl here, Thérèse, and she bears my child.

Claire halts and then resumes.

I am deeply sorry for the wrong that I have done you and your mother and for the further wrong I do when I ask you that she may not go destitute.

I understand that your mother may not be able to forgive me, but, Andrew, you must know your father for what he is and *know too that the love I have felt for Thérèse takes nothing from that which I feel for you. I hope that one day you might feel able to know your brother or sister and tell him or her that your father loved you both, more than anything in the world.*

I have not the words to say it all. Perhaps words are not enough, after all. I hope only that this will reach you somehow so that you will know your father thought of you every day, till the last.

Your loving father,

And here is his signature, sweeping bold, as if he had tried to say more with the gesture of his pen than the preceding sentences had been able to convey. Claire sits and stares at it for some moments. Then she folds the sheets slowly, replaces them in the envelope and reseals it.

'Where did you get this?' she asks quietly. 'Did he give it to you?'

I nod.

'He asked you to post it? After the war was over?'

I nod again.

She is silent again for a long moment. 'Why didn't you?'

I say nothing.

'Did my mother ask you not to?'

I shake my head.

'So why then? I don't understand.'

I take her hand in both of mine, turn it over carefully, not meeting her eye. I do not know what words to trace there.

'I was angry,' my fingers say.

'And are you still angry with him?' she asks.

'No,' my fingers say, and I shake my head as if to underline the words. 'No, I'm not'

I look up and see my face in the mirror, familiar and yet unfamiliar, too. I see her beside me, her expression uncomprehending. I stare at our reflections until the features become blurred, indistinguishable from one another.

And then I rise, taking the letter from her hands, go downstairs and then out, in the direction of the post office.

January, 1915

We stayed inside that day. My sister was restless, her eyes red and swollen flickering constantly to the door, as if James might appear there at any moment. The snow was still falling, less heavily now, but the frost had hardened it to iron underfoot.

Voller ate with us at midday. He was tense, distracted, consumed by the sound of the battle which had not abated, but raged on, the sound of guns oddly distorted by the snow so that they seemed closer. His eyes were on my sister too. He watched her: the way she moved about the room, the new hint of ungainliness in her actions, the thickness about her waist, her tear-stained face, red eyes. Once she turned and caught his gaze, but he looked away quickly.

'You are quiet,' she said, for the silence was oppressive that day.

'We have lost a lot of men.' He spoke low, without looking up.

She paused a moment before she said: 'Perhaps so too have we.' She waited for him to look at her.

He glanced up quickly.

'They were ready for us,' he said. 'The British knew exactly where the attack was going to come from. When it was coming. Our men just ran into their guns.' He looked down again. I noted the way his hands fumbled for a cigarette, although the food on his plate was unfinished. Usually, he asked my sister's permission before he smoked, but today he seemed oblivious.

'They were forewarned. They knew even where our gun emplacements were. Somebody told them.' He glanced at her again quickly. 'And you say there are no spies?'

My sister shrugged, her anger crushed by his. 'I don't know.'

'Of course. Nobody knows anything.' Normally softly spoken, there was a harshness to his voice now that I had not heard before.

He extinguished the barely touched cigarette clumsily so that it crumpled in the ashtray. Then he looked up. Saw that my sister was crying now, slow tears which she did not wipe away but let fall as she stared at her hands in her lap. Then he rose to his feet, his chair scraping harshly on the tiled floor.

'I'm sorry,' he said. 'Forgive my rudeness.' He stood roughly to attention, his face still pale but not with anger. I was reminded for a moment of the soldier in the bar, the one whose hands trembled so that he could not drink, the one who had killed his first man that day.

'Your family has shown me courtesy.' He did not look at me, but straight at my sister. 'I know that there are French wives, and mothers too, who have lost loved ones today.' He faltered, addressing himself still to my sister. 'In war, we all do what we think is best at the time. Perhaps, when all is known, we will feel differently. There will be time to reflect on right and wrong then.' He pauses again. 'But I have meant your family no harm.'

He bowed quickly towards my father, then turned to leave. At the door he stopped, hat in hand. He half-turned back into the room, hesitated, as if about to say something more, then halted. He turned back to the door and exited quickly.

September, 1932

It is maybe a month later that the letter comes. It is late September and the days are still bright with the dregs of the dying summer. I have forgotten, as I do every year, the colours of autumn and am startled anew by the russets, reds, golds that seem to set the landscape briefly aflame.

Claire is playing out in the square with the other girls, a skipping game, just like the ones I used to play as a child. She is taller than ever now, taller than her mother, but there is still a childishness about her bearing which I do not remember my sister having. I listen to them sing. The lyrics are different, but the game is the same, the bare legs leaping to avoid the rope that arcs over them and catches at their ankles.

The letter arrived this morning. We do not receive much mail here; Claire has received none before this. The postmarks and the stamp are English, her name written in looping, familiar script: Mlle Claire Winter. Not our family name, but his.

It is short, terse, dutiful in its acknowledgement of her as his half-sister. It makes no reference to her mother, or to his. It says that solicitors will be writing in due course, with details of a settlement for her. This is what their father would have wanted, he says. He writes *our father* and the short sentences suggest it cost a lot for him to write this. There is no reference to any intention to visit, no request for contact to be maintained. But it ends on the words *Your Brother, Andrew Winter* and he says he will write again. This, after all, is something.

I watch her through the window. It is Claire's turn now and she hovers outside the leaping arc of the rope, hesitating, waiting for the right moment to leap in.

'She will ask too, one day.'

I jump, startled. I had not been aware that my sister had come into the café. She is standing a few metres behind me, watching the game in the square.

'She will want to know what happened to him.'

I turn, look at her, bite my lip. Nod.

'She will ask her brother, I expect. And he will tell her, I suppose.'

Claire hesitates one more time, waits for the rope to turn another loop and then leaps in. The rope swings over her and the children chant as she starts to jump.

I know this is true. She will find out from

Andrew, or from Magali, if we don't tell her. She will find out about Henri Marcel, will wonder why no one ever reported him, why he is still allowed to drink here, in this café, the man who betrayed her father. She will ask all these things.

Perhaps Andrew will report him. Such things have been done, in other villages, close to here. Traitors have been brought to trial, even now, when so many years have passed.

I look at my sister. She is staring out at the square, where they are starting to count now.

'One — two — three — four . . . '

My sister has never asked me about the shapes I traced on her hand the day she found out James had died. She has never asked. And I wonder now if she knew what it was that I had said that day, if her hands felt the impress of my confession.

I think of what Voller said. He left the village before Claire was born, transferred to active service, at his own request. He wrote once, thanking us for our kindness, apologizing for repaying it so ill. He sent some money for Claire. He was killed at Arras in 1917; I saw his name on the casualty lists.

I think of what he said, that January:

'We all do what we think is best at the time,' and I wonder if it was intended for me, or for him.

Claire continues to jump outside in the square. The picture is bathed in gold autumn sunlight and the chanting grows louder as the rope swings higher and faster:

'One hundred and fourteen — one hundred and fifteen — one hundred and sixteen . . . '

She has a letter from her brother in her pocket and she jumps higher and higher. My sister and I stand side by side, watching her from the window.

We do hope that you have enjoyed reading this large print book.

Did you know that all of our titles are available for purchase?

We publish a wide range of high quality large print books including:
Romances, Mysteries, Classics
General Fiction
Non Fiction and Westerns

Special interest titles available in large print are:
The Little Oxford Dictionary
Music Book
Song Book
Hymn Book
Service Book

Also available from us courtesy of Oxford University Press:
Young Readers' Dictionary
(large print edition)
Young Readers' Thesaurus
(large print edition)

For further information or a free brochure, please contact us at:
Ulverscroft Large Print Books Ltd.,
The Green, Bradgate Road, Anstey,
Leicester, LE7 7FU, England.
Tel: (00 44) **0116 236 4325**
Fax: (00 44) **0116 234 0205**

Other titles published by
The House of Ulverscroft:

SAFE HARBOUR

Janice Graham

As Canon of the Parisian cathedral of St
John's, Crispin Wakefield has attracted a
devoted following, but also the jealousy of
his Dean. And the expensive indulgences
of his wife and daughters are threatening
financial ruin. Into this turmoil steps Julia
Kramer, international actress and childhood friend from Crispin's family home
back in Kansas. With her partner Jona
frequently away, Julia is drawn into the
cocoon of Crispin's family and his beloved
cathedral. Deeply indebted, Julia uses her
celebrity and wealth to promote Crispin's
career. When Jona's business dealings lead
him into deadly waters, Julia turns to
Crispin for support, igniting vicious
gossip . . .